LEGACY OF DESTRUCTION

LEGACY

BOOK TWO

DENISE CARBO

Editing: Red Adept Editing: Amanda Kruse

❀ Created with Vellum

For my Aunt Jane: Technically you're my husband's aunt, but in my heart you're mine as well. Your love of family and kindness always shines through in whatever you do. Thank you for always making me feel a part of your family. Here's the book you've been patiently waiting for!

Legacy of Destruction

What do you do when your own family is the greatest threat to your survival?

Willow, a psychic witch, has one dream—freedom. Now that it's within her grasp, she's on the run and ready to battle to the end for what she wants and those she loves.

Justin has one goal—revenge. Life has taught him some harsh lessons and trust no one is at the top of the list. The witch's captivating beauty and outrageous scheme won't deter him from his course.

An immortal evil hunts them both. Can they learn to stand together?

Magic always has a price. Will their budding love pay it?

CHAPTER
ONE

She was gone. His anchor, all he had left in the world.

Stale air and the taint of neglect permeated the small cabin. A fine layer of dust coated the furniture. She would have hated that. She'd never had much in the way of material possessions, but what she did have, she'd kept tidy.

Justin straightened the patchwork quilt on the bed, drawing it over the pillow where the indent of his grandmother's head still remained.

He hadn't been there for her final breaths, to hold her hand or ease her pain.

His fingers trailed over the quilt's soft, well-worn material. The framed photograph on the nightstand drew his gaze—a picture taken of him and his mother when he was a small child. It was the only photograph on display—the only one she'd kept. He'd tucked away a miniature copy in his wallet. He had only a vague recollection of when it had been taken. They'd spent the day at the beach playing in the surf and building sand forts—a rare day of carefree play.

A dog-eared copy of the Bible lay next to the frame. He'd asked her once why she still read it, why she still believed. After silently staring out the window for so long he'd thought she wouldn't answer, she'd replied, "It comforts me and provides wisdom on the days I have none."

His hands fisted at his sides. *Did it give her solace at the end? Did she read the words once again, seeking answers? Was an old book all she had to turn to in her final moments?*

Justin tilted his head back and closed his eyes. He hadn't been there to say goodbye.

The tension in the air built. A soft rumbling echoed beneath his feet.

His eyes shot open. Raw power filled the room. The hairs on his arms stood on end. Like a live current, the room zapped with energy. He took deep, labored breaths, trying to rein in the power, to draw it back into his body.

It was no use. He'd lost control.

Windows rattled in their frames. The picture fell from the nightstand onto the floor. He stared at the frame's cracked glass. A jagged line separated him from his mother.

Justin turned and strode from the bedroom into the main room of the one-bedroom cabin. A glass fell from the open shelving in the kitchen area and shattered. Dishes clattered against each other. One by one, glasses flew off the wooden ledges and joined their smashed brethren on the floor. The little bird salt and pepper shakers he'd given his grandmother as a belated birthday gift, bought with his first paycheck, lay broken on the red rug under the table.

The walls shook as the earth's resonating growl echoed around him. He rushed to the door. The handle turned in his hand, but the door was stuck in its shifted frame. Justin leaned his shoulder against the wood and shoved with all his strength, then squeezed through the slight opening.

The bright Mexican sun beat down on him as he slid from the cabin. The ground split beneath his feet, and he ran. A shudder moved through the earth, knocking him to his knees. He scrambled to his feet and sought open ground away from the cabin and the towering cypress trees around it.

A crack rent the air, and he whirled. The Mexican cypress tree toppled, crashing into the roof of the old cabin and rendering a giant hole. Creaks and groans rose from the tree and cabin. The wall gave a last shuddering attempt to stand before crumbling beneath the tree's weight.

Justin slid to the ground and rested his forearms on his drawn knees. Dirt and dust coated his skin and clothes. He coughed as his dry mouth and throat spasmed. It was like he'd drunk a dirt milkshake. He spat out the grime covering his tongue.

The quake ended after a few moments. The earth resumed its slumber, leaving him to stare at the aftermath.

His grandmother's cabin was destroyed—lost to him, just as she was. Her meager belongings were ruined because he'd lost control of the power he'd had since birth. A power he certainly hadn't asked for and didn't want. It had only brought him destruction and despair.

It had taken his mother from him.

After his mother's death, his grandmother had always kept them on the move. They'd never resided in one place for more than a few months. As a man, he'd continued the habit, but after a while, his grandmother had wanted a place to call home. She'd chosen the cabin and had lived there for the past five years. He'd visited, often at first, less and less as the years had passed. And he'd called to check in and make sure she had anything she needed, but he should have been there. She'd never said she was unwell, never hinted that her heart was giving out.

He hung his head. He was tired of running, tired of hiding.

Someone had murdered his mother because of the power that ran through their veins.

For generations, his family had been hunted. No more. Now he would do the hunting. He would find those responsible for killing his mother and finally make them pay.

He had nothing left to lose.

CHAPTER

TWO

Willow took a deep breath of the salty ocean air as she leaned against the metal railing of her brother's deck. The wall of glass facing the ocean behind her and the rest of the large modern home on the Connecticut coast fit Sebastian perfectly. She wasn't surprised he'd never taken her there before or even spoken of the private getaway. With a telepath for a sister, secrets were hard to keep. Miranda probably would've plucked the information from Willow's mind, who would then have been responsible for betraying her brother once again.

Waves tumbled onto the beach in a soothing rhythm. The only early-morning inhabitants were a man walking his dog and a woman jogging on the packed, waterlogged sand. The man threw a stick into the shallow waves, and the brown Lab bounded in after it.

A smile stretched across Willow's lips, and a chuckle escaped her. She would like to have a pet someday. But the hope was probably empty. The smile faded, and she looked away from the idyllic scene. Pets or caring too much about anyone or anything was a luxury she'd learned not to indulge in. It had been a hard lesson to learn, but

4

she'd learned it young. Sebastian was the only thing left that she cared about in the world.

Caring about anything or anyone was both a blessing and a curse. Her brother never showed it, but to him, it must be more of a curse. She was the leash around his neck. The tool their family used to keep Sebastian in line.

If she were braver and less selfish, she would've ended their suffering years ago. If she were gone, her brother might have a chance to escape their evil family.

Tears filled her eyes, and her gaze studied the blue-gray Long Island Sound stretched before her. She could walk into the water and just keep going. Eventually, her limbs would tire and the ocean might do what she'd never managed on her own.

Or it might spit her back out after dragging her along the rocky bottom for a while. That aligned more with her life.

She absently wiped the tear from her cheek. Crying was pointless. It changed nothing. It was as useless as she was—ineffectual power that harmed more than helped.

Cold seeped over her skin. Her gaze blurred. She clenched her hands around the cool, metal railing. The sounds of the ocean grew louder, stronger as a white haze descended over her vision. Strange barking came from a distance. It wasn't the dog from the beach, though. It sounded distorted. The waves crashed harder on the shore.

Beneath the scent of the salty air hung a thicker smell, like dirt and vegetation. The haze shimmered and dissipated. It was the ocean, but different. The waves were bigger, the water a deeper blue rather than gray.

Willow searched her surroundings as the vision strengthened. She knew she was seeing somewhere else. *But where? Why?* She would only have seconds to make sense of it. Her visions never lasted long. They teased her with snippets she had to interpret and untangle.

An empty beach. A seagull's call. She glanced behind her. A forest with towering trees. She gasped. They were colossal—not just tall, but wide at the base.

The barking came again. She whipped her gaze back to the sand.

There, on the rocks, down the beach. *Are those seals?*

A man came into view, tall, powerful—not just muscular. He had power. The white aura surrounded him and glowed brightly. The stronger the aura, the more power the witch had. At least, it seemed that way to her. Sebastian said he never noticed a difference in a witch's aura. They either had one or they didn't. His was bright too. Her brother was one of the most powerful witches she'd ever encountered.

She recognized the dark-brown hair and sharp features. Justin Crown. He scowled out at the ocean with his fists on his hips. She'd seen him in visions twice before, and both times he'd appeared angry. *Angry at what? Or who?* She never wanted to be on the receiving end of that anger. He'd caused an earthquake in the last vision she'd seen of him.

Her vision dimmed. Willow fed it power, hoping to make it last. She needed more information. *Is it now, the past, or the future? Why is my power so useless?*

The scene snapped away like someone had turned off a light and plunged her into darkness. She swayed.

"Easy." Hands clasped her shoulders and pulled her against a warm body.

She stumbled and blindly reached for purchase.

The darkness turned gray, then it brightened and cleared—like she had stepped from inside out to a bright, sunny day, and her eyes needed a few seconds to adjust.

Sebastian led her to a lounge and sat with her. "What did you see?"

"Justin Crown. He was on a beach, maybe California. It had giant trees—redwoods, I think. And seals."

"Why do you think you saw him again?"

Willow shrugged. Except for family, Justin was the only one she'd ever had more than one vision of. "Who knows? I don't know if it was now, in the past, or in the future."

"I'll get you some water. Stay here." Sebastian walked into his house through the sliding glass door.

She scooted over and lay back against the gray cushion. The vision had weakened her. They always did. *The price of power?* Using magic weakened her siblings too. But they were more powerful and did greater magic. She only had random visions she had no control over. Yet, it still sapped her strength.

"Here." Sebastian stood over her with a glass of water. His blond hair flapped in the breeze as he watched her with hazel eyes. Concern etched his face.

She gulped it down and closed her eyes once again. The healing power of her element spread through her like liquid energy. The lightheadedness lifted, and the lethargy left her limbs. She shielded her eyes and blinked at her brother, who sat on the lounge next to hers.

He waited patiently. Sebastian rarely acted impulsively, unlike their brother and sister. Miles and Miranda were volatile. They could be relatively pleasant one moment and, the next, send her flying into a wall or down the stairs for sport.

"Was he alone? No sign of our father?"

Willow shook her head. "Justin was alone as far as I could see. Hopefully, Father is still searching in Mexico." She'd told Edward, their father, about her vision of Justin causing an earthquake there, but she hadn't told him the vision had also shown her Justin had already left.

"Any sign he'd been in a fight? Could you tell if he still had his power?"

She frowned. "I didn't see any bruising. The vision was brief, and he was standing farther down the beach. He still had power, though, and a lot of it."

If Father had found him, he wouldn't have been able to steal

Justin's power without a solar eclipse. So her vision must have been the present or immediate future, because the next eclipse was only weeks away.

"Maybe the vision showed me where he is now or where he's about to be so we can find him and convince him to join us." They needed more witches on their side if they had any hope of survival. It was just a matter of time before their family located them. Sebastian's magical wards and legal shenanigans could only hide them for so long.

Sebastian gazed at her with a raised eyebrow and a drole look. "You think some sentient being is sending you visions to guide you? For what purpose?"

"I never said a being was sending me visions, but who's to say there aren't gods or goddesses? We're witches, after all. Most people don't believe in us either."

"If there are, then they either have a twisted sense of humor or they're as evil as our father. Why else would they let him continue to torture and destroy lives for his own gain?"

"Free will? People make their choices. I chose to tell Father about my vision of Justin to save myself."

"You told him to save both of us and give us time to escape."

Willow clasped her necklace and dragged the sea turtle charm back and forth across the gold chain. "I told him so he wouldn't torture me." She dropped her necklace and rubbed her chilled arms. The lick of flames still sizzled in her mind from the fire her father had threatened her with. The heat had reddened her skin as the fire had surrounded her. Sweat had poured down her temples and back. Smoke had filled her nostrils. She'd dry heaved and curled herself into a tight ball on the blackened bricks lining Edward's torture chamber.

Edward knew all her weaknesses. He'd been angry over Sebastian's failure to produce Josephine's heir. He'd threatened to kill Willow and Sebastian if he didn't get his way. He needed to sacrifice a witch during the eclipse to extend his life again. He should've died centuries ago.

She knew her days were numbered, anyway. Her father wouldn't hesitate to sacrifice her and capture a more powerful witch to join his coven so he could control them and use their power. Her vision had shown her that Cory Bishop could be that witch. She was Josephine's heir and powerful.

Willow winced. At one time, she might've let Edward sacrifice her. She'd gotten so tired of merely existing, surviving until her family doled out the next round of torture.

But her vision had also shown Sebastian and Cory uniting to defeat Miles and Miranda. It had given her a spark of hope. Hope for freedom. For herself and Sebastian.

"You must see by now that our only chance is to find powerful witches and form our own coven to defeat him."

Sebastian grimaced, walked to the railing, and leaned his back against it. "I see nothing of the kind. You and Coralea are engaged in a fantasy. Do you have any idea how long it takes to put together a coven? Look how long our father has been building one. To build one powerful enough to go against our family? It's delusional to believe that can happen in any beneficial time frame. He's weakest before the eclipse. We need to concentrate our time and energy on ways to kill him now or run like hell and stay as far away from him as possible. We can't waste time searching for powerful witches we might convince to join us. Witches are selfish creatures. Anyone powerful enough will be a problem. We might end up worse off—if that's possible. At least we're free right now."

Willow drew her knees into her chest and wrapped her arms around them. "Father never built a full coven because he keeps killing them off. I'm not naïve enough to think we can build a full, powerful coven overnight, but having you and Cory is a beginning. If we can convince Justin to join, that's four of us. Miles and Miranda might come around if they see potential. That would make six, which would put us halfway there."

Sebastian stared at her coldly. "You still hold out hope that Miles and Miranda will go against our father? Willow, you can't possibly trust them. Promise me you won't, ever."

"I don't trust them. I'm not stupid. But I don't discount that they might want their freedom as much as we do."

He rubbed his hands over his face and squinted up at the sky. "Miles and Miranda are self-serving to the end. They would sacrifice either of us in a heartbeat."

"You've threatened to do the same to them."

Sebastian dropped onto the lounge next to her. "And I would. I don't exclude myself from the selfish moniker. I'm just as self-serving as the rest of them."

Willow patted his knee. "You say that, but it's not true. You've put me first all our lives, and you saved Cory rather than handing her over to them. You could've just done what Father told you to do and located her. You didn't have to train her. You didn't have to fight them with her."

"You're the exception, but I would've turned Coralea over in a heartbeat to save my skin. I told her as much from the beginning."

"And that's another exception. Miles and Miranda wouldn't have been honest about their intentions. Justin might not be good. I don't know him. I've only seen him in visions, but I feel it in my soul that we should find him. Even if you're not ready to form a coven, we need to ensure Father doesn't get to Justin first and turn him or take his power. You see that much, don't you?"

"That much I can agree with." He looked out at the ocean. "You said the redwoods? By the shore?"

Willow nodded. "I know it's not a precise location, but it's a start. It gives us a general area to look for him."

"At least he chose somewhere near the water. I suppose we can be thankful for that. It would really put us at a disadvantage if we had to search for him in the desert, away from a water source."

"Way to look at the positive side, little brother."

He shot her a derisive look. "You're all of three minutes older than me, Willow."

"Yes, but I really love those three minutes. Don't try to take them away from me."

The bark of the giant tree he sat against dug into his back, but the slight discomfort felt grounding rather than repelling. The verdant-green underbrush was lush and plentiful. Justin scooped the rich, dark soil into his palm and let it trail through his fingers. The forest teemed with life. From the microscopic creatures to the skyscraping tall trees, life surrounded him. Yet silence echoed all around.

He'd gotten lost among those trees when he was a boy. He'd been playing and had wandered too far into the woods. It had all looked the same, and he hadn't known how to find his way back to the cabin he and his mother had been staying in. She'd been frantic when she'd found him sitting against a tree with his face buried in his arms. He hadn't cried. He didn't remember being afraid. He'd known his mother would find him.

He wished he'd known then how little time he had left with her. He could've made different choices. If he had, maybe she would still be alive.

Justin tilted his back against the tree. He'd returned to the forest not only because it was where his mother had died, but because it was the last time he could remember being genuinely happy and carefree. His grandmother had taken him and run from that point forward. They'd never stayed in one place longer than a few months. He'd kept a similar pattern when he became an adult. Only then had his grandmother settled in one place. The same place she was buried.

She'd never given him a straight answer about who or what they were running from. She blamed the mysterious "them" for his mother's death and others before her. He hadn't found any clues in her cabin before he'd leveled it. He had nowhere to start his search for revenge. Maybe he should've stayed in Mexico. Whoever hunted his family might've found him then, and he would have had the fight he thirsted for.

His grandmother and mother had both been terrified of anyone knowing about his power. Anytime it got away from him, they would run. They'd both had power from the earth, but theirs focused on plants, and they didn't have his volatility or strength.

They didn't cause earthquakes or create sinkholes that swallowed cars whole.

He'd been ten years old when he did that one. It hadn't been intentional. His powers rarely were. His grandmother had gone as white as a sheet and had stared at him silently for several moments before she'd herded him into the house where they'd been staying to gather their belongings. They'd disappeared that same day and had never gone back.

Justin took a deep breath of the clean air and stood. He wouldn't find answers sitting in the woods, ruminating over the past. The long fern fronds brushed his legs as he walked back to the cabin. He'd bought it from an older couple several years ago. They hadn't been the owners when he and his mother had stayed there. It had changed hands a few times before sentimentality had gotten the better of him and he'd purchased the place. He'd been careful to hide the paper trail. Nothing should lead back to his real identity, but buying the cabin had gone against everything he'd been taught.

The one-bedroom structure hadn't changed much in the past couple of decades. Owners had modernized parts of it over the years. At least he was comfortable. The roof was fairly new, and the appliances were from the current century, at least.

He scanned the surroundings at the edge of the clearing where the cabin sat. Trees enclosed the area. Only a narrow dirt path led to civilization. He couldn't even call it a driveway. Nature had done its best to reclaim the path over the years of his absence. If he decided to stay, he might clear and widen it into the driveway it once had been. Then again, it might be more secure to leave it inaccessible to vehicles—even his. He knew enough ways to escape that didn't include the path.

Nothing stirred in any direction. The closest road was half a mile away—a rough dirt track that barely met the definition of a road. He'd parked his Jeep at the end in a small dirt parking lot the forest constantly tried to reclaim. The closest paved road or house in either direction was several miles away. No sign of disturbance caught his eye.

Justin waited a moment more before stepping into the clearing and walking to the cabin's back door. His gaze continued to search.

It took less than a minute to check the interior. Except for the bathroom door, the layout was wide open. The bedroom sat in an alcove at the front next to the bathroom. He glanced at the ladder to the loft above the bedroom and bathroom. He'd stayed there as a child but would have to crawl to enter the space anymore. Anyone hiding up there would have to be fairly small. From his angle, he could see all but the corners of the back wall in the loft. It was empty.

He grabbed a glass, filled it with water, and drank as he wandered to the kitchen table and glanced at the papers strewn over the surface. Justin plucked an apple from the counter and tossed it back and forth in his hands. He didn't have much to go on. Nothing new had magically materialized since he'd looked it over a couple of hours ago. Copies of the newspaper articles detailed an unidentified woman's remains found on a beach and police reports investigating the unexplained homicide. The stack was thin. The trail had gone cold long ago.

He took a bite of the red-and-green apple. The cool crispness exploded over his tongue.

They'd never identified the woman as Maria Crown or any of his mother's many other aliases. They'd never found her killer, who'd burned her alive and left her husk of a body on the beach for scavengers to desecrate further.

Justin shoved the papers to the corner of the table. The police files had been surprisingly easy to hack into. Perhaps he should give it another go and check for updates. He might've missed an alert. He doubted they had solved the crime, however. He was fairly sure that would be front-page news.

He polished off the apple and chucked the core into the garbage can by the back door.

One of the burner phones rang—a Mexican number. The only one who had that number was the priest his grandmother had grown close to, who had handled the details of her death. Justin had given it to him in a moment of weakness or grief—he couldn't say which.

He connected the call but said nothing. He should've disposed of the phone days ago, but it still held a message from his grandmother. She had been the only one with that number before the priest.

"Mr. Alverez?"

Justin gave a soft grunt. He wasn't an Alverez and never had been. It was an alias his grandmother had used during the last few years of her life.

"I thought you'd like to know of some strange visitors I had yesterday. They were looking for the owner of your grandmother's cabin."

Justin clenched the phone in his fist.

"When I mentioned she had passed, they asked about a man she might've been associated with. You're the only visitor Anna ever had."

"What did you tell them?"

"I told them nothing, of course. I'm not in the habit of giving personal information about my parishioners to strangers. Just as the confessional is sacred, so is my knowledge. I told them as far as I knew, Anna had no one."

Is he saying my grandmother confided in him? Does he know about our past? Our secrets? "Thank you. What can you tell me about them? Did they say what they wanted? How many of them were there? What did they look like? Do you know where they went?"

The priest chuckled. "That's more words than I believe I've ever heard you speak. There were two of them, a man and a woman. The man was older, with a British accent. He walked with a cane and had glasses and a goatee. The woman was younger, with light-brown hair. She spoke little—just stared at me. It was a little uncomfortable, actually. Before they left, the man turned to her, and she shook her head. Oddly, he hadn't said a word, but it was like she responded to a silent question. They left, but I don't know where they went. It was a few hours later before I remembered I had your phone number."

Witches? His grandmother had told him a few tales of witches with unique abilities. *Could communicating silently be one of them?*

"Thank you for your discretion. I know what a comfort you were to my grandmother. I owe you a debt."

"There is no debt, my son. I hope I did provide some comfort to Anna. She spoke of you with great affection, and I know she loved you dearly. Be well, and I hope you find peace with your grandmother's passing. She is with God."

He would not argue theology with a priest, but he had a tough time believing anyone was watching out for him or any of the billions of people on the planet. If anyone deserved to have found peace, though, his grandmother did. "Thank you."

Justin said goodbye and dismantled the phone. He destroyed the SIM card. If the priest spoke the truth, they weren't likely to trace

Justin or even know of his existence. He had no reason to make it easy for them, however.

They possibly had nothing to do with those who had hunted them or killed his mother. They could be interested in something else, like purchasing his grandmother's land. The priest could've told them she'd left it to the church. But if that was all they were after, they would've said.

If they were looking for him, they would have a tough trail to follow. In the past, any inquiries into his whereabouts would've signaled it was time to move on. But he wasn't going anywhere. Let them come. The hunted had become the hunter.

CHAPTER

FOUR

The man sat on the beach watching the ocean. His broad back was to her, but the tug in her gut told her it was Justin Crown. His dark hair fluttered in the breeze. A wide cuff adorned the wrist he rested on his upright knee.

What is it about this man that affects me so? It wasn't his power. She'd been around plenty of powerful witches. He was handsome, but she had seen more attractive men who didn't tug at her insides.

Seeing him in her visions hadn't prepared her for the storm of feelings overwhelming her. *Why have I had multiple visions of him?* It couldn't just be her guilt from telling her father about him. She'd had to betray witches in the past to save herself and her brother.

Willow brushed her hair from her face. The high winds whipped it right back. She should call Sebastian and tell him she'd located Justin. He was searching the nearby town, but something had drawn her to the beach. At first, she'd thought she was drawn by the ocean and her element, but then she'd recognized the beach from her last vision.

Sebastian still wasn't convinced about forming a coven of their own. He also wasn't the friendliest person to outsiders—unless he chose to charm them. Her brother could be very charismatic when he wanted to be. The problem was he rarely did anymore.

His mood had turned sour after searching up and down the California coast for the past three days. Sebastian was more likely to fight with Justin than convince him they were allies.

Besides, it was her mess to fix.

Willow clenched and unclenched her fists. She trod carefully down the narrow path to the beach. The warm sun heated her skin, but the ocean breeze made it more than bearable. Sand filled her low sneakers instantly. She should've removed them.

Justin didn't turn or acknowledge her presence in any way. *Are the waves covering my approach?* Her feet dragged through the sand like a stomping buffalo's. *How could he not hear me?* She was about ten feet away from him. *Should I call out and announce myself?*

And say what? Hi there, interested in joining a coven of witches to combat an immortal evil who will probably kill us all?

"Finally decided to come down off the cliff?" He glanced over his shoulder, and his deep-brown gaze raked her from head to toe. His head tilted slightly as his gaze pinned her to the sand, one foot in front of the other as if she were frozen in place.

So he'd seen her standing up there, ogling him while she'd deliberated about approaching him by herself. *Lovely.* Off to a great start.

Willow cleared her suddenly narrow throat. "Yes, well, um…" *Speak like an intelligent human. He's going to think you're an idiot.* "Sorry. I didn't mean to stare or be rude."

Justin stood and dusted the sand from his behind. Her gaze tracked the movement. He folded his arms over his chest and stared at her silently. Her cheeks heated.

Great, he caught me staring again. She cleared her throat—again. It was not going well. Maybe she should've waited for Sebastian. She held out her hand. "Hi, I'm Willow."

He scowled and continued to stare at her.

Dropping her hand, she raised her other one to twist her necklace around her finger. She should've thought her plan through better. *Is he really so unaccustomed to people approaching him?* Sure, she'd been staring, but she doubted she was the first woman who'd ever ogled him. He was a handsome man. Maybe he was too used to it and wanted to make it clear he wasn't interested.

"I'm not trying to hit on you or anything. If that's what you thought." Willow closed her eyes briefly. *Am I really this inept at talking to people?* Her family kept her locked up most of the time, but it wasn't like she'd never conversed with anyone before.

He was still scowling when she opened her eyes.

This was a bad idea. He could probably kill her, and no one would be the wiser. Unless he caused an earthquake to do it. Sebastian would figure it out and avenge her. Then her family would probably find him and kill him too. All because she couldn't manage to string a few coherent sentences together.

"What do you want?"

He hadn't blasted her across the beach yet. *Does he know I'm a witch? Is that the problem?* She was, naturally, disguising her power to avoid drawing unwanted attention. They'd been taught from the beginning how to hide their nature from others. *Can he see through my attempts?*

If she wasn't honest with him, they would probably lose any chance of gaining his trust. If she was honest, he might kill her.

She should've called Sebastian.

"I mean you no harm. Not that I could cause you any even if I wanted to." She traced the edges of the sea turtle on her necklace and sighed. "Justin, can we start over?"

He dropped his arms, and his scowl deepened. He took two steps closer and loomed over her. "How do you know my name?"

She gulped and tilted her head back. "Um... I'm... I'm a witch. I have visions. I saw you."

His eyes narrowed. "Saw me how?"

"Well, see, that's complicated. I don't really know how to explain it."

"What did you see?"

"Oh, I saw you here on the beach. It's how I found you, actually."

"Why are you looking for me?"

"Because of the vision. I needed to warn you." Willow took a deep breath. "You're in danger. An evil witch is searching for you."

His gaze strayed over her features before he frowned and propped his hands on his hips. "Tell me what you know."

She rubbed her damp palms on her shorts. "He wants your power. He'll either try to make you join his coven or steal your power and kill you. The second one is more likely, though both are equally heinous."

"You saw all this in a vision and decided to track me down and warn me? Why? And don't try to tell me it's out of the goodness of your heart."

"No, it's not. I mean, I don't want him to find you. But I also have an ulterior motive."

"Which is?"

Willow tugged on her ear. "I want us to help each other. To stop him. If we formed our own coven—"

He slashed his hand through the air in front of her. "I work alone. I have no interest in joining a coven."

She stumbled backward a few steps. He could probably end her with a few swipes of one giant hand. *This plan might be my last. Not a great ending to my short life.* "You can't fight him on your own. He's too powerful, and he's not alone."

"Thanks for the information, but you have no idea what I'm capable of." He strode away down the beach.

Great, now he's leaving. Willow tripped after him. "I know exactly what you can do. I saw the earthquake you caused in Mexico."

Justin pivoted and stalked back to her. "What do you know? Were you there?"

She froze and wobbled in the sand, gaping at him. "What? No, I saw it in a vision."

He scowled and pointed his finger in her face. "What makes you think I would ever trust you? For all I know, you're working with this evil witch, as you call him. You said he's not alone. Prove you're not one of his coven."

The wind whipped her hair in her face. She stuffed the strands behind her ears and back into the remnants of her braid. *How much should I tell him?* Too much, and he would never trust her. Not enough, and he wouldn't give them a chance.

"How am I supposed to prove anything? I can tell you all you need to know about him. I'll gladly do that. Just listen to what I have to say. You truly can't fight him alone, and he *will* find you."

His gray T-shirt stretched across his chest as he fisted his hands on his hips and stared at her silently. He ignored the dark hair lashing at his forehead and cheeks.

Willow folded her arms over her waist and waited for him to make a choice. *How can I convince him of his peril? How can I prove he needs us as much as we need him?*

A seagull called overhead, and another swooped over the rocks down the beach.

Willow licked her dry lips. They tasted of salt from the ocean air. "I knew a powerful witch once—a kind one. Stacia could call a tornado. It was both terrifying and awe-inspiring to witness. He siphoned her power until the light, then the life, drained from her eyes."

Willow pressed her tongue to the back of her teeth until the tears dried from her eyes and the tightness left her chest. Stacia had shown Willow kindness when all she'd known was neglect and abuse.

"That is what you're facing. He has no goodness inside him. He only knows how to take and destroy."

Justin narrowed his gaze and studied her. "How do you know so much about him?"

The moment of truth. He might kill her for it. Or it just might make him believe her.

"He's my father." Willow tensed for his reaction.

Justin raised his chin and flexed his jaw.

Okay, he hasn't killed me yet. She held up her hands placatingly. "Biologically speaking. He was never a true father to me. I was simply another tool he created and manipulated to do his bidding. If he locates me, I have no doubt he'll kill me."

She'd betrayed him, and his punishments were absolute. The little use she'd been to him was gone without Sebastian in his clutches.

"Give me his name."

Willow sighed. "Edward Marks."

He spun away. She grabbed his arm. Power sizzled and arced between them.

She gasped and stumbled back. *What was that?*

He frowned down at her, his dark brows bunched together. He looked as confused as she was.

"Please, listen. He was on his way to Mexico looking for you the last I knew, but it won't take him long to realize you're not there."

"British guy?"

"What? Yes, originally. How do you know that?"

"Someone tipped me off that an old British guy and a young woman were asking questions about me in Mexico."

"That must've been Miranda. She can read minds. If whoever they talked to knows where you are, then they will too."

"No one knows. Except you." He stepped closer. "Are you going to tell him?"

"Of course not! Haven't you been listening? He'll kill me too. What can I say to make you believe me?"

"Not a single thing. Thanks for the information, though. Now I know who I'm hunting."

Willow watched him stride across the beach. *Is he crazy? Does he plan to hunt him on his own? After everything I told him?*

She went after him. The sand sucked at her shoes and hampered her movements. Meanwhile, Justin lengthened the distance between them as he walked across the beach like he was strolling down a road.

"Wait!"

He didn't pause or even look back.

She kicked off her shoes and ran. It could be her last chance to convince him to help them. If he disappeared, she might never find him again. But Edward would. Even without her, he always managed to locate other witches. Money bought information, and he had plenty of wealth to spend.

He stopped just as she reached him, and she slammed into the back of him before falling to the ground. Justin spun and scowled at her.

She raised her open palms toward him. "Please, just listen to me. It doesn't have to be this way."

A blast of power soared past her, and Justin flew backward.

CHAPTER

FIVE

The blast hit his side. Pain ricocheted through his body as he sailed backward and landed with a thud on his hip. Justin's gaze shot to a man waltzing toward him. He curled his fists, and the sand cascaded through his fingers. It looked like they'd found him after all.

Good. I don't need to keep hunting.

The earth rumbled as he jumped to his feet and threw his arms toward the man. He directed everything he had into a targeted shot. Power radiated up from the ground, through his body, and out his palms.

The man waved one hand and raised the other toward him.

Willow scrambled to her feet. "No! Stop!"

Justin's power bullet smashed into the man and sent him several steps back, but he stayed on his feet. A wave of water barreled into Justin and knocked him to his knees. The man was powerful, and obviously, water was his element. Justin concentrated on the ground at the man's feet. He needed enough power to disable the man but not so much as to cause an earthquake and possibly destroy lives and property. The sand swirled.

25

"Sebastian, stop! This is Justin Crown. He wasn't hurting me. I fell."

Justin's gaze shot to Willow then back to the man. *Sebastian?* Not Edward. *Who is he?* She hadn't mentioned anyone was with her. *Deceit? Had she lied?*

The sand sucked the man down, burying him to his knees as he sank. Sebastian shot a blast of power that hit Justin square in the chest. It made him step back and hurt like hell, but he held his ground. The shot was weaker.

Willow gasped and stumbled toward Sebastian.

Who is he to her? A lover?

She stood between them with her hands up. "Justin, please don't hurt my brother. He was just protecting me."

Brother? Justin's gaze flicked over him.

Sebastian was buried to his waist. Strain showed on his face as he fought the sand's pull.

A lethargy dragged at Justin's strength. An insidious magic battled his defenses and snuck through. Water rolled over the beach and encircled Sebastian and Willow.

"Willow, move," Sebastian growled.

She glanced out to sea, and her mouth dropped open. A giant wave rose from the ocean out of nowhere and surged toward them. The ocean roared.

"No, Sebastian. He'll drown!" She splashed through the water and threw herself at Justin. Her arms wrapped around his neck, and her legs clamped on his hips.

He gripped her waist and tried to dislodge her, but she coiled around him like a python. Energy flowed into him, restoring some of his strength.

Is she sending me power? Why would she do that? How is she doing it?

"If he drowns, so will I!"

The wave dissipated like it had never been there. Foam surrounded them as the water receded. Like a whirlpool, it spun around Sebastian's lower body as he used the water to dig himself out of the sand.

Willow remained wrapped around Justin. He glanced at the top of her pale-blond head against his chest. He could still feel gentle waves of power licking at him, lending him strength. He glanced back at her brother. He could blast Sebastian with power or use the sand to suck him deeper.

Why did she try to save me? He could've saved himself. He hadn't needed her help.

She raised her head, and wide blue-green eyes like the sea stared back at him. His hands tightened on her waist. A bright-pink blush spread across her cheeks, and she slid off him. She backed away a step and glanced behind her.

Sebastian stepped free of the sand and glared in Justin's direction.

The water streamed back to the ocean, tidal pools forming in its wake.

Willow scraped the wet hair off her face. "Sebastian, please. No more fighting. He could've attacked you again and didn't."

Her brother didn't spare her a glance as he strolled forward then stopped a few feet away. "Move away from him, Willow."

"Not until you promise to talk and not fight."

Sebastian stared at Justin. "You're powerful, but you lack control." He glanced at Willow. "You fed him your power, didn't you? I see the remnants all over him."

She raised her chin. "You would've killed him."

"You were on the ground with him standing over you. I was protecting you. How else was I to interpret the scene?"

"I told you, I fell. You could've stopped then."

"In the middle of a battle? You know me better than that." Sebastian turned his attention back to Justin. "You know she saved you, right?"

"You know I could have buried you beneath a ton of sand, right? You would've suffocated before your little water trick stopped me."

"Doubtful, but you would definitely have drowned. If Willow hadn't interfered and given you her power, you would've passed out and been dragged out to sea."

"Passed out? From what? Your little magic trick sapping my strength? I've felt worse after staying up too late."

Willow hung her head and sighed heavily. "You're both powerful witches who could easily kill one another. There, are you happy now? Are your fragile egos intact? Are you done with the male posturing yet?"

Sebastian cast a surprised look in his sister's direction. Justin grunted and folded his arms over his chest.

Willow glanced between them. "Are you ready to talk?"

Her brother brushed wet sand from his shorts and shirt. "Fine." He glanced at Justin. "You'll be dead soon." He gazed at Willow. "Probably would've saved him and us some trouble if you had let me kill him. Then we wouldn't have to worry whether a certain someone locates him."

"I already told him about Father. And no one has to die."

Sebastian lifted an eyebrow and continued dusting off his clothes.

Willow glanced between them and threw her hands in the air. "Can't you see? If we don't work together, then we've already lost and Edward's won."

CHAPTER

SIX

Willow dug her toes into the thick, wet sand. Her sneakers had washed out to sea. She would have to return to their hotel barefoot. That was hardly her most pressing issue, though. *How will I convince Justin and Sebastian that they need each other?*

The afternoon sun was high and already drying the sand Sebastian had drenched in water during his fight with Justin. Sebastian removed his shoes and dumped the sand out of them. It fell in wet clumps. He glared icily at Justin. The expensive leather loafers were ruined.

A slight smile twitched her lips at the absurdity of the situation. They were being stalked by an immortal evil who wanted their deaths, power, or both, and there they were, coated in wet sand, glaring at each other, and worrying about ruined apparel or their egos.

A giggle bubbled up her throat. She clapped a hand over her mouth as laughter burst out. Sebastian gave her an irritated glance while he continued to dig clumps of wet sand out of his shoes. Justin stood with his arms across his chest, ignoring the sand drying on his skin and the

29

torn shirt hanging from his body. It must've ripped during the fight. A tuft of his dark hair stood out to the side. Sand and a piece of seaweed poked out around it. Willow bent at the waist as laughter poured from her. Tears filled her eyes, and she gasped for breath. They both stared at her as if she'd lost her mind. Maybe she had.

She wiped the tears from her eyes as the laughter eased into chuckles and hiccupped breaths. "You both look ridiculous. This whole situation is ridiculous."

"You obviously haven't looked at yourself." Sebastian smirked and stuffed his soaked, sandy, sock-covered feet into his ruined shoes.

Willow glanced down at herself. Sand covered her front, probably from when she'd plastered herself against Justin. A tiny piece of seaweed peeked from the cuff of her blue shorts. She plucked it out with a smile.

Justin's gaze roamed over her. A warmth that had nothing to do with the sun spread through her.

She dusted off some sand and peered up at him from beneath her lashes. "Will you listen to what we have to say?"

He shrugged. "I'm still here. For the moment."

Willow sighed. "Okay." *Where to start?* "I'm not sure how to convince you or what you need to hear to understand how dangerous the threat is to you. To all of us. So I guess I'll give you a little information about our history. I told you that Edward is our father. Sebastian and I are twins. So are Miles and Miranda. They're our older siblings. Are you aware of how rare that is? Witches aren't very fertile. I don't know how he managed it or even if it resulted from his manipulations."

"You're veering off point, Willow. None of that matters." Sebastian put his hands in his pockets and jerked his head toward Justin. "What you need to know is our father is over three hundred years old. Immortal. He's manipulated magic and twisted nature to extend his life. Only he knows how, but he needs the solar eclipse and a great deal of power to work the spell. In short, he needs to drain a witch of their power. And you're the lucky sap he's chosen this time around."

Willow clasped her necklace in her fist. Edward hadn't chosen him. She had. "I'm sorry. I—"

"Yeah, yeah, we're both really sorry our father is an evil psychopath and that you're his current target."

She wasn't stupid. She knew her brother had cut her off deliberately to stop her from confessing her sins to Justin. He was most likely right not to divulge that secret just yet, while they were still trying to convince Justin of the imminent danger.

"Edward only has a few weeks until the eclipse." *When did I start to think of him as Edward instead of Father? Is it because I finally found some freedom?*

"What happens if he doesn't drain my power for the eclipse? Will it destroy him?"

"No, but it will weaken him considerably. He hasn't—for lack of a better word—fed for quite some time. He's already weaker than he's been in our lifetime." Sebastian bent and picked up a smooth stone. "He's a bit like this stone. The elements have worn him down." He turned it over in his palm. "Like these holes on the side, his power is weakened and fractured."

"If he's weakened, why not attack him now?" Justin asked.

"What would we do? Trap him in the sand? He'd fry you to a crisp in the blink of an eye, before you figured out how to control and direct your magic. You're erratic and unstable and no match for him or our siblings."

"Sebastian."

He held his arms wide. "What? Am I wrong?"

"Justin needs training, but he's one of the most powerful witches I've ever seen. He needs our help, and we need his."

Sebastian snorted and stuffed his hands back in his pockets. "We're wasting time."

Anger contorted Justin's face. He slashed a hand through the air. "His power is fire?"

Willow nodded warily. *What made him so angry?*

He cracked his neck. Power electrified the air. She glanced at her brother. Sebastian watched Justin carefully.

Please don't let Sebastian retaliate before I figure out what set Justin off. "What is it?"

"My mother was murdered. Her killer burned her alive."

She sucked in a harsh breath. "I didn't know. I'm sorry." Edward might not have been responsible, but chances were he was.

Willow clenched her fists and released them. "You could hide until after the eclipse. If you won't join us, at least do that. Edward will use someone else in your place."

Justin tilted his head and frowned. "Another witch?"

"Yes. If he finds us, it will likely be me. I'm the most expendable. So you can see why we're desperate for your help."

"He won't find you," Sebastian snapped.

"Running and hiding has never saved anyone for long in the past."

"He'd kill his own daughter?"

She looked at Justin. "Do you remember that witch I told you he killed, Stacia? She's the only one I've witnessed him show anything resembling affection. She was Miles and Miranda's mother. He killed her without hesitation when she tried to stop him from torturing a young witch."

Justin didn't need to know that the young witch was her. Edward had chosen Willow as a sacrifice once before, but Stacia had taken her place. One more reason her siblings hated her.

Justin ran his hands through his hair, dislodging the sand and seaweed. "What about your mother?"

"He killed her." Sebastian spun away. "Willow, I'll wait for you at the car." He stalked up the beach without looking back.

She closed her eyes. The knot of despair that seemed to be her constant companion surrounded her like a heavy blanket. Death and destruction followed her like malignant appendages she couldn't amputate. *Why does every decision I make bring about more inconceivable consequences?* Justin would never trust them or join them. *Why would he?* It would likely result in his death too.

"I'll give you one week." Justin stalked off in the opposite direction.

SEVEN

The trail narrowed the farther they walked. Trees loomed over them in every direction. Willow resisted the urge to check her phone again. Justin had spat his phone number as he'd stalked away and had told her to text him her number. He'd texted back directions and a time to meet.

Is he luring us to our deaths? Did I completely misjudge him?

Following instructions, they parked the car in a remote dirt parking lot and hiked the rest of the way in. It would be a prime spot to get rid of them. She glanced at Sebastian. His gaze surveyed their surroundings continuously. His arms dangled at his sides. He was prepared for an attack. He hadn't said much since they'd left the car, but he'd grown more tense as they'd walked.

"If anything happens, run, and don't look back. Get to the car. Don't go to the hotel."

"What about you?" Willow asked.

"Don't worry about me. I can take care of myself. I'll find you."

Meaning she couldn't take care of herself. She wouldn't bother arguing with him, but she refused to abandon him to save her own skin either.

The trail curved around a giant tree wider than she was tall. The forest opened to a small clearing, a meadow of ferns and moss surrounded by towering redwoods. She would think it quite beautiful if she weren't so worried they were walking into a trap.

They weren't alone, and she was pretty sure Justin was the only one nearby—the only witch at least. A non-witch might be lurking without her knowledge. For some reason, she had a harder time sensing non-witches.

Justin stepped out from behind another giant tree and sauntered toward them. Sebastian stepped completely in front of her and faced Justin.

Willow peeked around him. "This clearing is lovely but a tad remote. Why did you want to meet here?"

Sebastian scowled at her and shifted to block her once again.

"It's away from prying eyes," Justin said. "I don't think the locals need to witness whatever training you have in mind."

Willow stepped around her brother. "That makes perfect sense. Doesn't it, Sebastian?"

He merely glanced at her as he continued to survey their surroundings and watch Justin.

She rubbed her hands together. "Well, I guess we should start by asking what sort of training you've had. Were both your parents witches?"

"My mother had power, and so did her mother, my grandmother. I never knew my father, but he was normal, from what my mother told me. She died when I was a kid, so she wasn't able to show me much. My grandmother raised me, but she couldn't do the things I can, so she didn't understand my abilities."

"You're in luck. Sebastian has trained witches before. He trained Cory—"

Justin dropped, falling unconscious in front of her eyes.

She stared at him for a second before swiveling to her brother. "What did you do? Did you knock him out?"

"Yes. You need to stop sharing so much information with him. We don't know him and can't trust him."

Willow ran to Justin lying on the ground. She dug a water bottle out of the small backpack she'd carried in. He stirred, sat up abruptly, then swayed.

"Drink this. It'll help." Willow held out the water.

Justin glanced at her then the bottle. He flung out his arm and sent a shot of power toward Sebastian.

Willow's brother easily deflected it. "I train by doing. Attackers will not announce their intentions. You always have to be ready."

Willow touched Justin's shoulder. "Sebastian's power is water manipulation. He drained the water in your body. It's rapid dehydration. Drinking the water will help."

"I didn't drain much. You need to learn to deflect better."

"If this is how you trained Cory, I can understand why you're not her favorite person right now." Willow took the empty bottle from Justin. "Do you need another?"

Justin shook his head.

Sebastian glared at her as if he could silence her with a look. She supposed she should be thankful he hadn't rendered her unconscious too. Then again, he probably wanted to conserve his strength.

"Who's Cory? Another sibling?"

"No. She's—"

"Willow."

She ignored her brother's low warning and sent him a glare. "If we don't learn to trust one another, this is all pointless." She sighed and turned back to Justin. "Cory didn't discover her powers until she was an adult. Sebastian was sent to locate her." She waved a hand in the air. "Long story. Anyway, instead of handing her over, Sebastian trained her, and now, we're trying to form a coven to combat Edward."

"So, your father sends you to locate witches who he intends to drain of power and kill?" Justin asked.

Sebastian stuffed his hands into his pockets and glared back at Justin.

"He didn't have a choice. Edward used me to keep Sebastian in line. Sebastian only did what he did to protect me. He could've seduced Cory and handed her over to Edward, but instead, he trained her."

Sebastian sighed loudly. "If we're done with the history lesson, can we get on with the training? Time is not on our side. Willow, go stand out of the way."

Justin stood and cracked his neck.

Willow grimaced. "I just think—"

Sebastian flew backward and landed in the dirt.

Willow backed away swiftly. That was not how she'd envisioned the training session would go. Then again, she probably should have.

Justin's back slammed into a tree, and it shook from the impact. Willow scrambled to her feet and ran across the clearing when he didn't rise.

Troughs of dirt crisscrossed the clearing from both Justin and Sebastian sliding through the vegetation—often on their backs. They'd been at it for hours, and the only thing she could see they'd accomplished was to bruise and exhaust one another.

She fell to her knees beside Justin as he propped himself up against the tree.

"Are you all right?" she asked.

Justin nodded and kept his eyes on Sebastian as he used the tree to stand.

Sebastian stood in the middle of the clearing, his legs braced, his blond hair disheveled. Dirt and grass stained his pants. A hole in his shirt marked where he'd landed on a fallen branch that had pierced the cloth. He guzzled a bottle of water—the last one, if she wasn't mistaken.

"Must be a pain to transport your element with you. Not the same as being next to the ocean, is it?"

Sebastian lowered the bottle. "If you chose the clearing because you thought I'd be any less powerful, you clearly don't have a clue how my power works. You didn't take me to the desert. Water flows all around us. It's underground. It's in the trees and plants." He pointed to his left. "A stream lies less than a mile in that direction."

"Your brother is an arrogant asshole."

Can't really argue that. Willow sighed. "He's powerful, and he knows his stuff. He *can* teach you to control your power and direct it."

"Weren't you raised together? Trained together?"

"Yes, what's your point? I'm nowhere near as powerful as my brother."

Justin shifted his gaze from Sebastian to her. "You teach me. You don't piss me off—much. He does."

Could I train him? They didn't seem to be getting anywhere with Sebastian teaching him. And she'd gone through most of the same training growing up. Theoretically, she knew what to do.

Sebastian stalked toward them.

Willow stepped between him and Justin. "I'll do it."

Sebastian growled her name, "Willow."

She put up her hand. "Your way isn't working. I can do this."

Sebastian stared at her for a moment before turning his glare on Justin. "You harm my sister, and I'll end you."

"I don't hurt women. Isn't that your job? Seducing women and sending them to your father to be used and killed?"

Willow gasped.

Sebastian sliced his hand through the air, and Justin dropped like a rock once more. He wasn't unconscious, though. The earth heaved beneath them. Sebastian fell to his hands and knees. Justin climbed to his feet as the ground rumbled. A branch snapped and fell, hitting the dirt with an echoing thud. A crack opened in the earth. Dirt, rocks, and plants slid inside.

Willow stumbled, and Justin grabbed her, tucking her behind his back. He backed them against the tree, sandwiching her between his wide back and the harsh bark. She wrapped her arms around him from behind. His chest rose and fell with rapid breaths.

She placed her palms flat on his chest. "Stop. You need to focus. Shut it down. Let the power building in your body dissipate. Breathe. In and out. Calm yourself. Imagine the magic flowing out of your body and floating away without causing any harm. You can even imagine the power encased in bubbles. Pop each one until the magic is gone."

Justin glanced over his shoulder at her with an incredulous expression.

She shrugged and smiled. "Whatever works."

The ground stopped shaking. The trees quit shuddering. He let out a harsh breath, and his body trembled from the effort. Willow stroked his chest. The magic energizing the surrounding air dissipated.

Sebastian stood. His gaze ricocheted from her to Justin then to where her hands still petted his chest. She stopped and dropped her arms. Willow gently shoved Justin forward so she could step out from behind him. She could still feel the grooves from the tree against her back.

"Same time and place tomorrow?" She pasted a smile on her face and looked at Justin.

He stared at her as if she'd asked if they were traveling to Jupiter. "I'll send you an address."

"Great. See you tomorrow." She grabbed her brother's arm before he could say or do anything to aggravate the situation and dragged him across the clearing to the path.

When she glanced behind them, Justin had disappeared into the forest. She thought she got a peek of his aura, but she wasn't sure. Her senses told her he was moving away from them.

They reached the car, and Willow took a deep breath of the fresh air. "Cory would probably love this place. Can you imagine the magic she could wield here? We should probably call her and check in. Don't you think?"

Sebastian pulled his arm from her grasp. "Be my guest. I have nothing to say to her or that numbskull she's attached herself to."

"Finn is hardly a numbskull, Sebastian." Handsome as sin with a devilish smile was how she would describe him.

"You hardly know him. I can't comprehend what Coralea sees in him."

"Why do you still insist on calling her Coralea instead of Cory?"

"It's her name."

"She prefers Cory and has said so more than once."

Sebastian smirked slightly and shrugged.

"You do it purposely to annoy her, don't you?"

"It's the small pleasures in life that sustain me."

Willow glanced at him. He'd dated her briefly, but that had only been to discover if she was the witch he was looking for. *Right?*

"Sebastian, did you have genuine feelings for her?"

"Don't be ridiculous. She was simply a target then a tool."

"I know you don't really feel that way. If you did, you would've turned her over to them instead of teaching her to use her magic."

"I used her to help us."

Justin's words must've pierced her brother deeper than she'd thought. She knew what guilt felt like and how it burrowed inside and carved a permanent well of sadness and shame.

"If that's true, then why did you arrange for her aunt to go on an extended cruise and help Cory and Finn go into hiding? You didn't have to."

"Father still could have used Coralea to restore his power. It was pure self-interest to send them away."

"Keep telling yourself that, but I know better. You have a heart, brother, and it actually cares about people."

"It only cares about you. Be careful around him, Willow. Don't let down your guard. People will always disappoint you."

CHAPTER

EIGHT

Justin watched Willow exit the passenger side of the car. He'd been clear that he was only willing to have her instruct him alone. Her brother was too interested in demonstrating his supposed superiority to teach him anything. He doubted Sebastian had any real intention of helping him learn to control his power. He didn't seem to share Willow's determination that they needed to unite to fight Edward Marks.

Edward Marks. He finally had a name to attach to his hatred.

He had no doubt Edward Marks was responsible for his mother's death and the reason Justin had spent his entire life running.

Willow stood next to her brother, nodding. Her pale-blond hair cascaded down her narrow back in a loose ponytail. He couldn't deny she was a beautiful woman. She didn't hide behind makeup or flashy outfits. Her clothes were simple but probably cost more than the majority of his wardrobe.

He was too far away to hear their words, but Sebastian was clearly lecturing her or trying to convince her of something. Justin had texted her directions to his cabin the previous night. The remote location meant they had little to no chance of anyone stumbling upon them accidentally. He would know if anyone intentionally approached his property as well. He was extending her some trust in divulging his location. *Hopefully, it won't prove to be a grave mistake.*

The doubts had led him out there that morning to watch for her arrival. Perhaps, deep down, he'd known they wouldn't follow his instructions for Willow to come alone.

Justin glanced away from their discussion and toward his cabin. He could make it back there, grab his go bag, and disappear before they got close. His mother and grandmother had taught him from an early age to keep a go bag with his essentials packed and ready to go at a moment's notice.

Sebastian cast a look around the woods. His gaze paused where Justin hid.

Can he detect me? He'd hidden inside a fallen tree.

Sebastian may possess some power to reveal him. Justin frowned. He simply didn't know enough about magic beyond what his mother and grandmother had told him.

Sebastian shifted his gaze and got into the car.

He's leaving?

Willow backed away from the car and walked over to the trail toward the cabin. Maybe her brother had just given her a ride. He probably didn't want to be without a car while they trained. So, she *did* follow his instructions.

Justin kept pace with her as she traversed the path. He'd given her directions for the longer route just so he could track her. He also wasn't entirely sure their car would make it to where he'd parked his Jeep.

She seemed oblivious to his presence, even when he closed the distance between them. He walked through the woods almost parallel to her path. Her gaze remained on the ground ahead of her. She didn't glance right, left, or behind her.

Justin frowned and veered toward the path, stepping onto it about fifty feet behind her. Willow didn't glance back or show anyone sign that she knew she wasn't alone.

Does she have no concern for her safety? Anyone could catch her unaware. Has no one taught her to be vigilant of her surroundings at all times? Has her brother taught her nothing?

For that matter, what was Sebastian thinking letting her meet a man she barely knows in the middle of the woods alone? If she were my sister…

No, she wasn't his sister. His attraction to her was not the least bit brotherly. His gaze lingered on the way her long legs strode down the path and the slight swing of her hips. He shoved the feeling aside. Just because she was beautiful and he was attracted to her didn't mean there was a chance in hell he would act on it.

"Are we going much farther, or are we just out for a stroll in the woods?"

His gaze rose from her backside to her slightly tilted blond head. *So, she did know I was here. For how long?* "I was beginning to think you had no concern for your safety. How long have you known I was behind you?"

She stopped and turned to him. "You've only been behind me for a short time. Before that, you were tracking me in the woods." She nodded to her right, where he had, indeed, been following her.

Willow gazed up at the tops of the trees before glancing back at him. "I learned from an early age to be aware of my surroundings and any danger nearby. I knew you were there when I stepped out of the car."

"Is it a spell? Or does it have something to do with water being your and your brother's element?"

"No, it's not because of my element. Well, at least, Sebastian and I don't share the same abilities. I sensed your presence. I can generally feel others nearby, especially witches. Once you moved from your hiding place, I could see your aura in my peripheral vision." She wrinkled her nose and pursed her lips. "There is a spell to detect magic nearby, but I don't recall the specifics. Sebastian probably knows it. I can ask him for it."

"Auras? Do you mean the glow that sometimes appears around a witch when they work magic?"

"Is that the only time you see them? Do you not see an aura around me right now?" She frowned. "Well, mine isn't very strong because I'm not powerful. Did you not see Sebastian's? Oh wait, Sebastian doesn't see differences in witches' auras either. But he does see their power auras."

Justin grimaced and crossed his arms over his chest. *Is this another ability I lack?*

Willow approached him. "When I look at a witch, I see what I call their power aura. It's like a glowing outline of their body. The more powerful the witch, the brighter it is to me. For instance, both yours and Sebastian's auras are very bright."

"Regular people don't have auras to you?"

"Oh, yes, they do, but it's not the power aura. The power aura sparkles. Regular people don't have sparkles. They have muted colors sometimes, but generally, their auras are shades of gray or beige. I can't be sure, but I think it's because people are never all good or all bad. Obviously, some are worse than others. If I concentrate and look closely, I can detect a witch's element. The power aura has a slight color outline. Water is blue. Fire is orange. Air is yellow. Yours, earth, is green."

Justin nodded. That would be a helpful power to possess. If he could tell someone was a witch, how much power they had, and which element it came from, he would have a strong advantage. "You have a powerful ability."

Willow frowned and shook her head. "Oh no, my powers are pretty useless. I'm a liability. It's why Father kept me away from battle."

"Are you sure he didn't keep you out of battle to protect you and your abilities? You have visions of the future. You can identify other witches and how strong their powers are. You can also see exactly what element they draw their power from, which tells you what magic they can wield."

Willow stared at him as if none of that had occurred to her before. *Did she really believe she's useless?*

"If you know a witch's magic originates from water, then you know they can either wield water, connect with marine life, or have the power of premonition like you. If you see they possess earth magic, they connect with animals, control plants, or manipulate the ground like me. For fire, you'll know they can wield actual fire, have the power of healing, or mind control. Then there's air, which bestows weather, telepathy, or telekinesis. I'd say that gives you and anyone on your side a powerful advantage." His mother and grandmother had taught him about witches and the different magics they could wield. Unfortunately, when it came to his specific magic and how to wield his power, they didn't have enough knowledge or ability to help him. At least he hadn't been completely clueless about magic.

She suddenly grinned, and her entire face lit up as if she glowed from within. "So, you're saying I've convinced you to join us?"

His lips twitched. "Nice try, but no."

Willow frowned and sighed. "Then I suppose we better carry on with training. Maybe that will sway you." She glanced over her shoulder at the path. "Exactly where are we going? Another clearing?"

"My cabin."

"You live out here?"

"At the moment."

"It's beautiful. Humbling too."

"What do you mean?" He began walking, and she fell into step beside him.

She waved her arm at the forest surrounding them. "Look around. It's so awe-inspiring. Not just the height and width of the redwoods. It's the sheer majesty of everything in the forest working together in some form of synergy. If you think about all the unique landscapes on Earth, you can't help but be amazed by how life differs but works together in perfect balance. Don't you think?"

"I can't say I've ever thought about it that way."

"No? Take your element. Cory's power is plants. She said she sees the energy and plants connecting each other and everything around them like microscopic highways. Is it the same for you?"

Justin gazed around them. "I don't know what she sees. It's more of a feeling for me. I can sense the earth below us and tell you the sedimentary rocks nearby. It's what made me so good at working on the pipeline or in the mines."

"Wow, that's interesting. I had no idea you could do that. Sebastian can always sense when water is nearby and how much. I can, too, but to a much less powerful degree."

"My mother and grandmother both wielded the power of plants. They could make anything grow. My grandmother once told me a fanciful tale about a witch who could use trees to travel from one place to another—like portals."

Willow looked at him with her mouth open. "You're kidding."

"I thought it was a fairy tale or a children's story. But when I asked her to retell it when I was older, she said it wasn't a story. It was real."

"Cory will love that. Imagine if it's true!"

NINE

Willow stared at the phone ringing in her hand. *Why's Cory calling me?* She'd texted a couple of times to check in but never called before. Willow glanced around the bedroom of the rental unit they'd moved to from the hotel. *Did something happen? Did my family go after Cory again when they couldn't find Justin?*

Staring at the phone wouldn't deliver any answers, so Willow shook her head and answered. She hesitated and bit her lip. *What if it's not Cory? What if someone has her phone and is using it to track me and Sebastian?*

"Willow?"

She let out the breath she wasn't aware she'd been holding. It *was* Cory. Unless someone could disguise their voice and make it sound like her. *There are devices or programs that do that, aren't there?*

"Willow, are you there?"

"Um, yeah, hi." The paranoia would be the death of her.

She'd been so excited when Sebastian had handed her the phone a couple of weeks ago. Her first. In the past, she had never been allowed to have one. Sebastian had snuck her one once, years ago, but her father had found it, and they'd both been punished severely.

She'd never thought it could bring about more anxiety and complications. *Should I ask some questions to confirm Cory's identity?* It wasn't like they knew each other well enough to know any deep, dark secrets about each other.

"Is everything, okay? I thought it would be nice to check in by chatting instead of by text. And I'd much rather speak to you than your brother."

Willow could understand that. Cory remained put out with Sebastian over the whole deceiving her and her aunt about his identity and intentions. "Yes, everything's okay. What about with you? They haven't found you or anything, right?"

"Nope, no sign of them. Aunt Addy is on her extended cruise, and Finn and I are taking a long road trip."

"Good. I was worried when you called instead of texting."

"Oh, sorry. I should've thought of that. When you didn't speak, I thought maybe you didn't want to talk to me."

"Oh, no, that's not it at all. I've never had a phone before, so I'm still getting used to it, then I had this paranoid thought that it might not really be you but someone pretending to be you. I'm sorry. My anxiety can be a little much sometimes."

"Don't apologize. You're right to be cautious. I should've thought of that too. We should have a code word or phrase or something so we know it's us."

Willow walked to her bed and sat cross-legged. "That's an excellent idea. What should we use?"

"Hmm, not sure. Let me think for a minute. Have you really never had a phone before?"

Willow twirled a strand of hair around her finger and frowned. "I wasn't allowed."

"I bet having so many new freedoms you were never given before can be a little overwhelming."

You have no idea. Just choosing a meal was new. Under Edward's rule, every dish was planned without her input. Her entire day had to be accounted for and approved. Willow sighed, nodded, then rolled her eyes when she remembered Cory couldn't see her. "It sure can. Sometimes, I almost have a panic attack over simply deciding what I want to eat." Willow cringed. She probably shouldn't have shared that. Cory would think she was crazy.

"I can only imagine what you've been through, Willow, but it sounds pretty reasonable to me that you have some serious adjustments to make. If you ever want or need to talk, I'm here. I guess it's not like you can pop into a therapist's office and tell them you're a witch and come from a family of evil witches."

"I think they'd lock me up and throw away the key."

"Therapy only works when you're completely honest. Having to hide what you are and lie about most of the details would be counterproductive and exhausting," Cory said.

"I've read a lot of psychology books over the years and even took some online courses. Theoretically, I know how trauma and long-term mental and physical abuse can manifest, but it's hard to apply coping methods to your own life sometimes." Willow frowned and picked at the comforter covering the bed. "It's like how it's always easier to give someone advice than to practice it yourself."

"Totally get that. My friend Mel will say something to me that completely nails it on the head about what I'm going through, and I'll be like, why didn't I see that?"

It must be nice to have a friend to talk things over with. Willow had never been allowed friendships. Even her online interactions were monitored.

"Hey, I know what our code word can be—freedom. What do you think?"

Willow smiled. "Perfect."

"I think so too. I went through a period after my divorce when I had to redefine and discover who I was and who I wanted to be. Then there was the whole finding-out-I'm-a-witch thing. You don't need to have all the answers at once or figure it out on your own. I know I could sure use a fellow witch to help me navigate this whole magical world I never knew existed. How about we lean on each other?"

"I'd really like that."

"Awesome. On that note, how do you control your powers when you're angry? Finn and I were having a...discussion the other day, and I was stalking away—rather spectacularly, mind you—when he called out to me all soft and hesitant. If you knew him well, you'd know Finn is rarely soft-spoken or hesitant. I glance over my shoulder to find him staked onto the ground and held down by vines. I had no idea I'd done it. I didn't even remember thinking anything magical. I felt awful and a bit terrified. What if I lose my temper and do something really bad?"

Willow stared out her window at the glimpse of ocean she could see. Magic always had a cost. And a witch had to be vigilant at all times not to unleash their power unwittingly.

"My powers don't seem to be tied to my emotions. At least, they never responded when Edward tried to trigger my visions using fear or anger. I think certain powers, like yours, Sebastian's, and Justin's, which manipulate the elements, can be linked to emotions. Once, when we were little, Sebastian burst all the pipes in the house after losing his temper."

"How did he learn to control it?"

"I'm not sure, but I think it helps to have something to focus on. I used to hold his hands and sing him silly nursery rhymes. Later, as he matured, he found his own balance." Willow smiled. She hadn't thought about those times in a while. They'd only had each other to lean on.

"It's hard to picture your brother as a little kid. He gives off the impression he was never inexperienced or immature, that he innately knew how to wield and control his powers. He's pretty emotionless."

Willow leaned back against her headboard. "He's really not. He's just had to learn not to show them. In our household, weaknesses were exploited."

"Don't expect me to feel sorry for him. I'm not ready to forgive him—yet. I don't want to picture him as a vulnerable little boy." Cory sighed loudly. "Damn it! Now I'll have to, won't I?"

"I know I've said it before, but Sebastian was only following orders to protect me."

"I realize that, and it's not like I expect him to put my welfare or my aunt's before yours. It'd be a lot easier to forgive him if he apologized and didn't act like such an arrogant ass about the whole thing."

"Sebastian can come across hard and unfeeling, but I believe he genuinely cares for your aunt and you. I doubt he'll ever apologize to you, though. In his mind, he didn't do anything wrong. He was protecting me."

A clicking noise came across the line like Cory was tapping her fingers on the back of the phone. "I get it. I still don't like it, but I get it. Tell me about this Justin character. Do you think he'll help us? Join us?"

Willow told Cory about finding Justin and everything that had led to her training him instead of Sebastian.

"Doesn't surprise me in the least. Sebastian's method of training leaves a lot to be desired. I don't miss the bruises after every session."

"He's a firm believer in learning by doing, but he and Justin just butted heads too much to be effective."

"Sounds like Justin has a greater problem with control than I do. And he's known he's a witch all his life?"

"Yes, but he was kept isolated, always moving from one place to another. His mother and grandmother share your type of power rather than his, so they didn't know how to help him."

"They have my power? Could they teach me? I still feel like I'm floundering in the dark half the time."

"They're both gone. He did tell me a story his grandmother told him about your type of power, though. She said a witch was so powerful that they could use trees as portals to travel from place to place."

"You're joking! Damn, that would be convenient."

"I don't know if it's true. I've never heard of anything like it before, but I'm sure there's plenty I haven't heard about."

"You're the closest thing to an expert I've got."

"Then you're in trouble."

Cory laughed. "No, I think I'm pretty lucky. I could be trying to figure it out on my own."

"Think of what we could learn if we find more witches willing to join our coven and stand against Edward."

"Right now, it's hard to think past defeating him before he destroys us. But I do agree that forming a coven to stand against him is our only hope of beating him. I don't want to spend my life on the run. And I can't keep sending Aunt Addy on cruises. She's bound to get suspicious."

"I know. Sebastian isn't sold on the coven idea yet, and neither is Justin. Frankly, I'm still surprised Justin agreed to work together at all. He hasn't committed to anything long-term. He only gave it a week, which is already half over. He's incredibly powerful and managed to control it even after Sebastian intentionally made him angry."

"How?"

"I used touch to focus him, then talked him through calming himself using breath. He's aware of when his power is getting away from him. He just needs to focus and keep it under his control. He's already making amazing progress."

"You like him."

Willow reared her head back. "Why wouldn't I?"

"I mean you have feelings for him beyond concern for a fellow human being. Are you attracted to him?"

Her cheeks heated. *Am I that obvious?*

"Willow?"

"He's handsome. It's kind of hard not to notice."

Silence stretched over the phone. It sounded like Cory started to say something but stopped. "Willow, now that we're friends, I want to ask you something, but I don't want to overstep or offend you in any way."

Willow lifted her knees closer to her chest and wrapped her free arm around them. She could guess what Cory wanted to ask. "Go ahead."

"Have you ever been in a relationship with a man before?"

She glanced at the bedroom door. Sebastian had gone out for supplies and was due back soon. The last thing she wanted was for her brother to hear about her lack of experience with men. But she was also dying to talk to someone. Miranda had never been the type for sisterly gossip fests. She'd been a tormentor rather than someone to confide in.

"No. I didn't have much opportunity to form relationships with anyone, let alone have a boyfriend."

"Okay, so have you... um, well, has anyone talked to you about...?"

"Cory, are you trying to ask if anyone has had the sex talk with me?"

Cory half laughed, half sighed. "Pretty much."

"No, but I've read a lot of books. I know how it works."

"Okay, good. Whew, I don't envy parents right now. If it ever comes to that with Finn and me, he'll definitely be the one who has to have the birds-and-the-bees chat with our kids."

Willow chuckled. "How are things going with Finn?"

"Pretty wonderful, actually. He can be infuriating. Still, I love him, and he makes sure I know he loves me too. But don't change the subject. We were talking about you and Justin."

"Were we?" Willow slid the sea turtle pendant back and forth along her necklace chain. "Just because I'm attracted to a man for pretty much the first time in my life doesn't mean I've forgotten all of our lives are in danger. I know nothing can become of it. Besides, it's not like he feels the same way."

"Willow, you're a beautiful woman. I'd be pretty shocked if the thought hadn't crossed Justin's mind too. I think the fact that our futures are so unpredictable is more reason to take a chance. We don't know what tomorrow will bring, so we have to live today and appreciate everything we have." Cory snickered. "That doesn't mean I'm telling you to jump in bed with him. Though my friend Mel probably would tell you to do exactly that. Just don't let our troubles hold you back from experiencing life."

Willow tilted her head back and stared at the ceiling. Cory made an excellent point. It might be her one and only chance to experience a lot of things. She wasn't ready to make the leap to having sex with Justin, but she wasn't exactly opposed to having her first kiss either.

TEN

The ground rippled, and Willow stumbled into Justin. He grabbed her upper arms and steadied her against him until the ground settled. Maybe he was being optimistic—not his strong suit—but he seemed to be grasping control of his power quicker.

Justin stared down at the top of Willow's blond head nestled against his shoulder. Their week was up. He'd given her the ultimatum, and he meant to keep it. She had helped him improve, but she and her brother hadn't earned his trust.

Willow stepped back with a small smile before she dropped her gaze. Her shyness around him had seemed to increase the past few days rather than decrease. So had her blushes. He rather liked the pink tinge on her cheeks.

He propped his hands on his hips. Willow was beautiful, but she wasn't his type. She was the date-and-get-to-know type, not the one-night-stand-and-scratch-a-mutual-itch type. So he wouldn't act on his attraction—even if it might be mutual.

"You're getting better."

He nodded and glanced around the clearing behind his cabin.

He'd successfully moved rocks and heaved the ground enough to flip a boulder, but he'd also almost toppled a tree and broken a window with a branch. "I've still got a ways to go."

"We'll keep practicing. You'll get it." She rubbed her palms together. "If you want to keep going, that is. I know you said a week."

Sebastian had kept his distance. He still dropped her off and picked her up every day. Justin waited for her to arrive then walked her to the car each time. And Sebastian always glared in Justin's direction.

He didn't plan to run anymore. The cabin was as good a place as any to stand his ground. If Edward Marks and the rest of Willow's messed-up family came looking for him—and he really hoped they did—he needed to be ready. He also needed to be prepared if they didn't show up, because he had every intention of taking the fight to them.

"The training has helped, so if you want to keep teaching me, I'm willing to learn."

She grinned. "It's not like I have anywhere else to be. I'm still holding out hope you'll join us."

"I've told you before, I'm not a joiner."

She nodded and wrinkled her nose. "Trust is hard to give or earn. I totally understand. Sebastian has been pretty much the only person on the planet I've trusted for a long time. But I'm willing to learn to trust others. I feel I have to—we have to—if we want to end this once and for all and stop running and hiding. I don't know about you, but I really do want a chance to live without looking over my shoulder."

Justin stared up at the towering trees bordering the clearing. He hadn't trusted anyone besides his grandmother since his mother had died. He'd moved from job to job and had kept his distance and his head down. He was tired of running, and what she offered was appealing. If she or her brother were to be believed, then he would never defeat Edward on his own. He would need help.

He rubbed the back of his neck. "I'll think about it, but I make no promises. Your brother doesn't seem on board with the whole work-ing-together idea."

"Sebastian knows we're stronger together and that will increase our odds of success. He'll team up to defeat Edward."

People could join forces without fully trusting one another. Justin had worked in plenty of precarious positions before in the mines and even on the pipeline. He had to trust the guys on his team enough to have his back and work together. It didn't mean he expected them to put their safety ahead of his. People were inher-ently selfish creatures. It wouldn't be much different if he decided to work with Sebastian and Willow. They would always put each other first.

Justin clocked the sun above. "We have a couple of hours left. Let's get back to it."

"Okay. Do you want to try spells again?"

He frowned. Reciting spells made him feel foolish. She'd brought a list of a dozen or so the other day. They'd been moderately success-ful, but he doubted it had resulted from the spells themselves. His grandmother had used spells from time to time.

"I've never really understood the point of muttering a bunch of words together," he said. "The magic doesn't come from words. It comes from inside."

"You're absolutely right. They're just words until your power gives them magic. Spells are another tool. Some witches use them extensively, and others not at all. They help focus your power and concentrate. If your mind is busy repeating a spell, then it's less likely to wander."

"I think it does the opposite of making me focus. I'm too worried about remembering and saying the words in the right order to concentrate on the power portion."

"Okay. Then we won't do the spells. Like I said, every witch is different. How about we try the holes again? I really think if you can open a pit to drop your opponents in, it'll be a useful surprise attack in battle."

Justin nodded and rolled his shoulders. He stared at the spot in the center of the clearing and envisioned a pit big enough for a man to fall into and have a hell of a time climbing out of. Power built in his core like a whirlpool of magic. He cracked his neck to the side, raised his hands parallel to the ground, pointed toward the target.

Energy coursed up his torso and out of his hands. The ground rumbled. A circle of grass disappeared before his eyes. Dirt swirled deeper and deeper.

Willow gasped next to him and jumped in the air. She clapped her hands. "You did it."

He released a breath and dropped his arms. He'd made a hole. *But how deep did it go?* A shallow trench might make an opponent stumble or even fall, but they would get right back up. He stepped closer.

The pit went down at least ten feet and had a six-foot diameter. Other than a couple of roots sticking out of the sides, nothing would aid someone trying to climb out. If he could just fill the pit on top of whoever he fought, he would gain even more advantage.

He raised his hands, picturing the hole filled and returned to its previous state. Sweat dripped down his back. The ground shook. Dirt rose in a column and settled, releasing a cloud of dust into the air. The grass had disappeared, and a perfect dirt circle remained.

"That was amazing. I knew you could do it." Willow grabbed his arm and beamed up at him. Her blue-green eyes were alight with her special inner glow.

He cupped her cheek. *One kiss wouldn't hurt anything.* He lowered his head.

She gasped and gripped his arm tighter.

His lips met hers. A zing of pleasure zapped down his spine. She was so sweet. His lips brushed hers again. Their breaths mingled, and he gently angled her head for a deeper kiss.

Willow trembled.

He opened his eyes and gazed down at her.

Her eyes were wide and luminous, her lips plump and dark. A blush stole across her cheeks. She was exquisite.

One *more* kiss couldn't hurt either. He lowered his head.

"Wait." Willow pressed her hand against his chest. "I have to tell you. It was me. I'm the one who told Edward about you. I told him about my vision."

CHAPTER

ELEVEN

Tears filled Willow's eyes as she listened to Justin stomp into the woods behind her. His expression had closed off completely, and he'd walked away without a word.

She wrapped her arms around her waist. *What could I do?* She had to tell him the truth. *I couldn't let a romantic relationship begin with a lie between us, could I?*

Justin had kissed her.

She'd had her first kiss, and she'd ruined it.

Willow slid to the ground, her hands on her knees. Tears spilled down her cheeks. He would never trust her after that. She'd ruined everything. Once again, she was the one to screw everything up.

How can I tell Sebastian? He'd warned her not to tell Justin.

No. She had to explain—make Justin see that at least he had to work with Sebastian and Cory. She scrubbed the tears from her cheeks. If he didn't want her around anymore, she would go. She wasn't powerful enough to add much to the coven anyway. She climbed to her feet and followed Justin into the woods.

There was no trail. He hadn't taken a path. Willow stopped and searched the trees all around her. A tug in her core turned her gaze to the right. There. He'd gone in that direction. She weaved through the giant trees. Delicate green ferns brushed her legs. Every few minutes, she stopped and refocused her senses on Justin. He'd turned twice so far. Most likely, he was deliberately evading her, ensuring she couldn't follow him.

She didn't blame him.

One of her power's few uses allowed her to track witches, a secret she'd kept from her awful family. She didn't understand exactly how it worked but guessed it had something to do with the way she saw a witch's aura—as if she could not only see it but feel it as well.

She sensed the water before she heard it. A stream stood ahead with a waterfall. The splash of the water greeted her as it joined the pool of water below.

Justin sat on an outcropping of rock above the waterfall. He didn't glance in her direction. He just stared down at the water, but she knew he sensed her presence.

Is it a good sign he's not blasting me back down the hill I just climbed? Did he realize I won't give up, or has this been his destination all along? Willow wrung her hands. *How can I fix this?* She took several steps closer.

His gaze turned and stopped her in her tracks. Anger poured from him. If he acted on it, she would probably be dead. Her hand brushed the rough bark of a nearby tree when she reached out for support. She laid her palm flat against it and took a deep breath as tears threatened once again. He hated her. It was what she'd always feared and what had kept her silent for so long.

"I'm so sorry. I know it's no excuse, but I was trying to protect Sebastian and, if I'm honest, myself."

He didn't say a word. He just continued to stare at her.

"Please don't let this stop you from joining Sebastian and Cory against Edward. I don't have to be a part of it." She shrugged. "I'm not a valuable member anyway. You'd all be stronger without me. I always intended to give my spot up when a more powerful witch could fill it."

Justin looked away.

Willow hung her head. She couldn't say or do anything else to convince him. Sebastian had told her to keep her mouth shut. "I'll go. But please don't give up on working with them. I honestly believe it's the only way."

Her throat spasmed with a sob as she turned and made her way back down the hill. She slipped twice on the needles coating the forest floor and fell to her hands. Tears coursed down her cheeks once again.

She stopped and leaned against a tree. Her eyes closed, and a shudder shook her. She clasped her hand over her mouth to stifle the sobs. Recently, she'd cried more than she had in years. She scrubbed her hands over her face and clenched them into fists at her sides. *Crying never solved a damn thing.* It only led to more pain and suffering—usually at the hands of her family.

Willow pushed off the tree and opened her eyes. She took a step forward then paused. She looked right and left, then behind her. The trees all looked the same. She'd been following Justin's aura or magic trail or whatever it was that told her which direction to go to find a witch when she'd entered the woods. But she had nothing to follow to find her way back to the cabin.

Great job, Willow! You're lost in the woods.

She dropped her head into her hands. *Could I navigate back to Justin?* She might still be able to sense the waterfall. *And then what? Ask the man who just found out you betrayed him for help?*

He was more likely to lead her deeper into the woods or off a cliff.

My phone! It had GPS. That could lead her out. Willow yanked it out of her pocket. *Please have a signal.*

She frowned at the dark screen and pushed the button on the side. *Why isn't it turning on?*

Oh no, did the battery die? Did I forget to charge it again?

Panic seized her chest.

What do I do now? How could I be so stupid to not mark a trail?

No one else in her family would be dumb enough to get lost in the woods. Miranda would've plucked the directions from Justin's brain. Miles would've fought him for them or maybe scented something in the air that would've led him back to the cabin. Or he would've used the wind and blazed his own path. Not that either of them were likely to follow anyone into the woods to apologize.

Sebastian would've known to watch the signs on his way in. He was always a cautious planner. She couldn't sense water as effortlessly as he did, but maybe if she could pick up another stream, she could follow it out to a road or something. Or maybe she could sense the well behind the cabin.

Willow slowly turned in each direction. She felt the pull of water behind her, but she was fairly sure that was the waterfall and stream, which had flowed in the opposite direction of the cabin.

She took several steps forward. *It has to be in this general direction, doesn't it?*

Cory could probably talk to the trees or something and figure out which way to go.

Willow glanced at the tree next to her. It was wider than she was tall and probably hundreds of years old. "Any chance you want to direct me toward the cabin?"

Nothing. Not even a rustling branch in response.

"Didn't think so." She tugged on her necklace. "Here goes nothing," she muttered and continued walking in as straight of a line as she could manage over the rough terrain.

Justin would probably find her dead body in a week or two while out on a hike or something. *Would he take the time to bury me?* No, he would probably step over her and leave her corpse for the wild animals to gnaw on—if they hadn't already, by that time.

Sebastian would be pissed. He would search for her. Probably kill Justin because he would blame him. Then he would blame himself for letting her train Justin alone. She couldn't let that happen. She had to find her way out of the woods.

Several moments later, she stopped and rested against a tree while she studied her surroundings. Nothing looked familiar. She closed her eyes and searched for water. She could no longer sense the stream or waterfall behind her. At least she thought it was behind her somewhere.

Her head tilted as she sensed something below the ground to her left. *An underground stream?* It was deep and faint. And better than nothing. Willow followed the winding trail of water beneath the ground.

The darkness below the canopy of trees gave way to light ahead. *Could that be the clearing? Did I trace an aquifer to the well?*

She stumbled over a root and fell. Dirt coated her pretty much from head to toe. She looked like she'd decided to roll down a muddy hill.

Brushing off her hands, she hauled her sore body to a stand. Some sort of clearing was definitely ahead. *Please let it be the cabin.*

Willow trudged on to the edge of the woods. A sigh left her, and she leaned against a tree. The familiar cabin sat in the middle of the clearing. Thirst scratched at her dry throat. She would kill for some water. *Well, maybe not kill. How much more pissed would Justin be if I broke into his cabin for some water? Probably not a good idea.*

She really wished she had Sebastian's abilities and could manipulate the water to flow to her. He could probably tap that well easy peasy. Maybe she could find an outside faucet to use.

She saw no sign of Justin. He hadn't returned before her.

Willow scanned the back and visible side of the cabin for a spigot. And stopped. A witch was nearby.

Did Justin return, after all? She spun and searched her surroundings. *No, it's not Justin.*

Sebastian. Her brother's presence was familiar and comforting—usually.

What time is it? Am I late? Oh no. She'd really hoped she would have time to clean up and think of an explanation.

He walked around the side of the cabin. His gaze swept over her and the surroundings. A storm of anger moved across his features. "I'm going to kill him!"

"No! Sebastian, he didn't do anything."

"Then why are you covered in dirt and God knows what else? You look like you've been dragged from one end of this forest to the other." His gaze continued to catalog her as he stalked forward.

"I wasn't dragged. I fell... a lot. It wasn't his fault. It was mine. I got lost."

"Where the fuck is he, and why were you wandering the woods alone?"

"Can we please just go back to the rental house, and I'll explain everything? I'm exhausted, thirsty, and starving."

Sebastian threw out his hand. The well cap popped off, and a stream of water floated through the air to her. The continuous stream splashed onto the ground between them.

She bent forward and drank. When she had her fill of the replenishing water, she splashed some on her face to wash away the sweat, tears, and whatever else she'd accumulated during her trek. "Thank you. I really wish I could do that."

The water dropped to the ground.

"Start talking, Willow."

"Everything was going great. He's gaining good control of his powers. But my conscience got the better of me, and I confessed I was the one who put Edward on his trail. He was understandably upset." She wasn't going to share the part about the kiss.

Sebastian stiffened.

"But he didn't do anything! He just stalked off into the woods. I was the idiot who followed him to apologize then got lost. You can't blame him."

"Watch me."

She grabbed his arm as he strode past her. "Sebastian, please. He didn't do anything. How would you feel if the situation were reversed? You would've lashed out at anyone who confessed to betraying you. You probably would've killed them. He did nothing to retaliate."

Her brother scowled at her then stared into the woods.

"We need him. You know it's true."

"I don't know anything of the kind."

Willow squeezed her brother's arm. "Basty, please."

Sebastian frowned. "You haven't called me that in a long time."

"Yeah, well, you haven't called me Willy in a long time either."

At some point, they'd both stopped using their childhood nicknames for each other. They'd developed something of a secret language to combat Miranda's telepathy. Maturity might have had something to do with it, but Sebastian had changed once he'd been given the freedom to leave unescorted. She'd felt left behind for a long time.

Sebastian sighed and pulled her into a hug. "Are you sure you're okay?"

She nodded against his shoulder. "Just tired, like I said." Her stomach growled. "And really hungry."

He dug the car keys from his pocket and held them out to her. "Do you think you can drive back to the rental?"

Willow stared at the keys and snatched her hand back without taking them. "By myself? Why? What are you going to do? Sebastian..."

"I'm just going to have a chat with him."

"No." She wasn't an experienced driver, but she knew enough to drive the car back to the house they'd been renting. He didn't need to know that, however. She would play the weak little sister if it meant he would return with her and leave Justin alone.

"Willy."

"Don't you Willy me, not now." She tucked her hands behind her back. "I can't do it. You know I don't have a driver's license. I'm not competent enough to drive all the way back by myself."

"We both know that's not true. I taught you to drive myself, remember?"

She did. Their father had forbidden her from taking the same driving education course as her brothers. Edward had antiquated ideas about women, and it was one more way to control her. Sebastian had gotten his license then taught her on one of the secluded roads of their estate. He'd been severely punished when someone had tattled on them. She'd been locked in her room for a month.

He sighed. "I just want to talk to him. You're the one who wants us to work together. How will we do that if we can't even have a conversation?"

"You promise you just want to talk?" Willow folded her arms. "I'm not leaving unless you promise not to hurt him."

"I promise." He held out the keys again.

CHAPTER
TWELVE

The darkening forest reflected his mood. Justin trudged back to his cabin, staring at the ground. Willow had betrayed him. She wasn't the innocent person she portrayed. He knew better. No one was innocent. He'd let his guard down, and once again, he'd gotten burned. He couldn't believe he had actually considered joining them—trusting them.

Justin stepped into the clearing, and his knees weakened. He slapped his hand against a tree and hung his head as his vision blurred and grayed. He knew that feeling. He should've had his guard up. His distraction would be his death. He called on his power as weakness brought him to his knees.

How could I have misjudged her so badly?

Sebastian stepped into the edge of his vision. "Be thankful I promised Willow I wouldn't hurt you. As long as you don't sport any bruises, I can keep my promise."

Justin's vision swam. His power deserted him. His strength gone, he fell prone on the ground.

Sebastian squatted next to him. "Now, you and I are going to have a little chat."

Justin squinted. Sebastian's form flickered before him like the power short-circuiting on a screen.

"Blink twice if you understand what I'm saying."

Did he say he wanted to chat? He's not here to kill me?

"Shit," Sebastian mumbled. He disappeared.

Was he an illusion? Or am I simply too weak to focus?

Water splashed in his face.

"Drink."

Justin stubbornly sealed his lips until the splash of water became a torrent aimed at his mouth.

"We can do this the easy way or the hard way. Your choice. Personally, I'd love nothing more than to drown your ass. But I like to keep my promises to Willow."

Willow made her brother promise not to hurt me? He hadn't imagined that part. Justin opened his mouth then gagged as water poured in and down his throat. *Is the asshole trying to waterboard me?*

The flow of water dwindled then cut off.

Justin collapsed onto his back. His vision had steadied, but his limbs shook and refused to support him.

"There, that should be enough for a proper conversation. Cooperate, and you can have more."

Is that supposed to be an incentive?

Justin glared as Sebastian, who once again squatted beside him. At least he wasn't flickering like a distorted image anymore.

"Your strength will return as the fluids in your body replenish."

Justin turned his head away and stared up at the blue sky. Evening approached. The sun would dip below the trees soon. *How long will it take for my strength to rebuild?*

"You have no right to be angry with Willow."

Justin refused to look at Sebastian. He was done with them both.

"We're all tools to my father. Willow's ability to locate other witches and her visions kept her chained to his side. He rarely let her out of his sight. She never went to school. She never had friends. She was rarely allowed off his property. If she failed to perform, she was punished. Should she have allowed herself to be tortured to save a witch she didn't know? Our father used us against each other—constantly. Should she have protected you instead of me—her brother—her twin? Would you have done any differently if you were in her place?"

Justin stared at the pointy tip of the treetop above him. *Why should I believe anything either of them say? Had she really been kept prisoner her entire life? What the hell did he mean she was tortured? Why is their evil bastard for a father still alive?*

He scowled. He shouldn't care.

But what would I have done differently? He would have done his best to kill the bastard. Barring that, he would've done anything to protect his grandmother. His mother.

"She only gave him your name and location once she knew you were no longer in Mexico. She never intended for him to capture you. Willow only distracted him to save Coralea and me."

Justin gave Sebastian the side-eye. *Why is he telling me this? What does he care if I understand her motives?* He opened his mouth. His dry, scratchy throat spasmed, and he coughed. He felt trapped in the middle of a desert instead of a lush forest.

Water splashed over his face and down his throat once again. He glared at Sebastian. *Where the hell is the water coming from?* His gaze landed on his well and the missing cap a dozen feet away. At least he knew it was clean.

"Why...?" His voice cracked, and he tried again. "Why are you telling me this?"

"She's got it in her head that the only way for us to defeat our father is to work together. I'm not a huge fan, but damned if I can see another way. I'm man enough to admit I can't do it on my own. Are you? Because I promise you, you don't stand a chance."

Justin looked away. Streaks of purple and navy streaked the sky. The weakness was leaving him. The water had helped. But the earth was restoring his powers. Lying prone like that connected him to his element. He felt energy flowing into him. He could probably draw enough to blast Sebastian across the clearing.

What would be the point? He wasn't at full strength. A fight would only assuage some of his hurt pride and provide an outlet for his anger. As much as Justin hated to admit it, Sebastian was right. Willow's plan to form a coven to fight Edward Marks was the smartest course. *But can I trust them enough?*

"I told her not to tell you. I knew eventually she'd give in to the guilt she was drowning in and confess to you. I did think she'd wait until you decided to join us. But then, she never could stand remorse or the shame that comes with it." Sebastian sat a few feet away from him. "Willow got all the goodness. She's my conscience. What's left of it, anyway. Make no mistake. If it comes down to you or us, I'll hand you over on a silver platter. Not Willow. She always puts others before herself. Now that she knows you, she'll never betray you—not even for me. You can trust her to do the right thing to the best of her ability."

"Why should I trust anything you say?"

Sebastian chuckled. "You shouldn't. But you can trust Willow. Probably Coralea, too, since she has that same moral code buried inside her. Mine was ripped out of me a long time ago, if I had one in the first place."

Am I a fool to believe him? "Where is she anyway?" Justin angled his head to look behind them at the cabin but saw no sign of Willow. Shadows lengthened at its sides. The sun hid behind the tops of the trees.

"That's another thing we need to discuss." Sebastian narrowed his gaze.

Does he know about the kiss? Is he about to go big brother on me?

"Care to explain why you allowed my sister to get lost in the woods? She came stumbling out covered in filth, exhausted, and she'd been crying, damn it. Willow doesn't cry anymore unless she's been pushed past her limits. You told me you didn't hurt women."

Justin winced. *She'd gotten lost? She'd been crying?* "Was she hurt?"

Sebastian looked at Justin like he was the stupidest person on Earth. "Did you not hear a word I said?"

"I heard you, but was she injured?"

"No. Other than a few scratches, she seemed physically fine."

Justin sat up with a low groan and draped his arms over his raised knees. "Where is she?"

"I sent her back to the rental to get cleaned up and rest. She was starving."

Justin rubbed his hands over his face. It hadn't occurred to him she would get lost. She'd found him easily enough.

"You're back to full strength, aren't you?"

Justin dropped his hands. *Is he asking because he wants to fight? What happened to his promise to Willow?*

Sebastian cocked his head. "You recovered quicker than I predicted." He looked down. "Does the earth replenish you like water does for Willow and me?"

"Yes. How do you not know that?" *Isn't he supposed to be an expert on magic?*

Sebastian shrugged. "Doesn't seem to be the case with all the elements. At least not with the witches I've known. I'm not sure it works that way with Coralea either. I'll have Willow ask her if she's noticed."

"You can't ask her yourself?" Both his mother and grandmother felt energized by the earth as well. Perhaps not to the degree he did, though.

Sebastian looked off into the woods. "I'm not one of Coralea's favorite people at the moment."

"Shocking."

Sebastian gave him the side-eye and stood. "Why haven't you tried blasting me with power or sent the ground rumbling under my feet? Willow's lessons must be helping more than she conveyed."

Justin climbed to his feet. The lethargy was gone. Sebastian's water trick no longer weakened him. "The thought did cross my mind. It would only provide a temporary satisfaction, though, so I refrained."

Sebastian slid his hands into his pockets as if he didn't have a care in the world. "I don't know about temporary. I still want to beat the hell out of you for upsetting Willow."

"Understandable. For what it's worth, that wasn't my intention. I never thought she'd get lost."

Sebastian's expression darkened. "I'm not sure her tears were from getting lost. I told you my sister no longer cries. Fear alone wouldn't do it. Certain members of our family got off on inducing fear. As a child, Willow was afraid of the dark. So they locked her in closets, trunks, the basement, all without a single source of light. Until I was old enough and strong enough to protect her. As far as I know, she hasn't cried in years. Tears waste precious water—our power."

Rage surged inside Justin for the little girl she'd been and what she'd endured. The ground rumbled.

"You care about her." Sebastian studied him like he might a lab rat he wanted to understand.

Justin frowned, and the earth quieted.

"Don't hurt my sister again. If you do, no promise I made will keep me from annihilating you."

"Don't threaten me. I'll bury you so deep in the ground, you'll suffocate before you find a drop of water to manipulate."

"So, we understand one another?"

"Perfectly."

THIRTEEN

Willow's nerves were stretched thin. *How will Justin treat me? Will he be cold and distant like when we first met? Or has my betrayal made him angry and disgusted?*

Sebastian had arrived back at the house after dark. He hadn't looked like he'd been in a fight, and he'd insisted it had been an amicable exchange. She doubted that they'd relaxed over beers or anything, and she found it difficult to believe they hadn't argued. But her brother insisted Justin understood and wanted to continue training.

How is that possible? Had Justin managed to deceive Sebastian? Is he waiting even now for me to arrive so he can kill me?

She pulled over and stopped the car on the shoulder of the narrow two-lane road. Maybe she was an idiot for insisting Sebastian not accompany her that morning. She'd thought it better not to tempt fate and had wanted to keep the two of them apart until they were fully on board with the coven strategy. Sebastian had barely argued about driving her, and she'd thought she'd scored another independence victory.

A horn beeped. She jumped in her seat as a car drove by, giving her the stink eye.

Willow sighed and pulled back out onto the road. Her only options were to face Justin and accept whatever he chose to dish out or go back to get Sebastian and use him as a shield.

No, it's time for me to grow up. Sebastian couldn't be her shield forever. It wasn't fair to him.

She clenched the steering wheel as she turned onto the narrow dirt road leading toward Justin's cabin. *Will he be waiting in the woods to escort me down the path like always?*

She parked in the dirt lot and stared into the woods where he usually waited. He wasn't there. She hung her head. Her door opened, and she gasped. Justin squatted in her open door and stared at her. His gaze roamed over her before returning to meet her gaze. He didn't look angry.

"Are you all right?"

Am I all right? Why would he ask that?

"Your brother said you got lost in the woods."

"Oh, that." Her cheeks heated. She dropped her hands into her lap. "I managed."

"I'm sorry."

She blinked. *Why is Justin apologizing to me? Has Sebastian developed some sort of mind control or memory wiping power I'm unaware of?* "You have nothing to apologize for. I'm the one who wronged you. I'm the one who should be sorry. And I am. More than I can possibly express."

"I know why you did it. I would've done the same."

"You would?"

He nodded, stood, and held out his hand.

This is a dream, isn't it? There was no way Justin was truly that understanding or forgiving. *Why is he being so kind? Is it a trick?*

She bit her lip and slid her hand into his. The men in her life attacked when she least expected it. They lured people into a false sense of security then knocked them to their knees in a surprise stroke. *Is that Justin's play?* Willow locked the car behind her and peered at Justin next to her. *What does he intend to do to me?*

"What is it?"

She flung her hands out to the side. "If you're going to blast me with power or bury me in a hole or landslide or something, I wish you'd just get it over with."

Justin frowned and folded his arms over his chest. "I'm not going to do any of those things. I told you I understand why you did it."

Willow rubbed her damp palms on her black shorts. "You're truly not angry?"

"Not going to lie. I was. Surprisingly enough, your brother made me see that you didn't have a choice. You were in an impossible situation."

The tension tightening her shoulders deflated. *He truly forgave me?*

The corner of his mouth hitched up in the semblance of a smile. "Ready for more training?"

She nodded absently and walked beside him down the path to the cabin. *All the anxiety that's been churning inside me since yesterday was for nothing?*

"Why are you being so quiet? Are you upset about getting lost in the woods? I won't let it happen again."

Willow blinked at him. *He thinks I'm upset with him? And how could he make sure I never get lost again?* She sighed. He thought she was too weak to take care of herself, like everyone else in her life did. "I'm not worried about getting lost. I'll be more careful in the future, and I did find my way out on my own."

Justin nodded. "If that's not what's bothering you, then what is it?"

She pushed a twig out of her way and peeked at him from the corner of her eye. "I guess I find it hard to believe you're not angry and that you're not luring me into a false sense of security so you can attack when I least expect it." *There. What does he have to say about that?*

"Is that what you're used to? From your family?"

"Yes."

"I promise I'm a hell of a lot more direct. When I'm angry, you'll know it. I'm not exactly great at hiding it." He chuckled. "I guess I don't try to either."

"Okay." Willow gave him a small smile.

Her gaze fell on his exposed wrist. He wasn't wearing his leather cuff, and it revealed a raised circle with a design inside. She peered closer. *Is that the Earth?* "Is that your power mark?"

Justin glanced at her and followed her gaze to his wrist. He nodded as he lifted his arm and looked at it. "Yeah, it kind of sticks out, so I cover it when I'm out in public."

"I've never seen one like that. Cory is of the earth, and hers is a tree, which makes sense since she controls plants."

"My mother and grandmother each had a flower on their ankles. It was in the same spot but on opposite sides."

"I wonder what determines the shape and location. I mean, other than it symbolizes a witch's power. If they had the same power as Cory, why wasn't theirs a tree too? And Cory's is on the back of her neck."

"You said she's powerful, right? Maybe it has something to do with the level of magic a witch has. My mother and grandmother weren't all that powerful."

The small cabin came into view as they rounded a curve in the path. The sun reflected off the large front window. Surrounded by the forest of towering trees, the cabin resembled something out of a fairy tale.

"That makes sense, but I don't think that's it because I'm certainly not powerful, and I have a raised eye." She stopped in the clearing and folded the top of her shorts down to show him the mark on her hip. "See? I was told once that the most powerful witch who shared my power also had the eye. It was an endless source of ridicule growing up—that I shared the mark of a powerful witch."

Justin traced a finger over the mark on her hip. A delicious shiver danced up her spine.

"They and you underestimate your magic. You're powerful. Your magic isn't the showy kind, but that doesn't make it any less formidable."

Willow bit her lip as a warmth spread out from her core. He continued to trace lazily over her mark. His gaze raised from her hip to her face. The breath stuttered in her chest. She'd thought she'd ruined any chance of a romantic relationship with Justin before it had barely started, but he gazed at her with desire.

His hand grasped her hip, and the other lifted to cup her cheek. His thumb brushed over her lower lip before his head lowered, and he kissed her. She gripped his wrist in her hand and returned his kiss. When his tongue sought entry, she couldn't help the startled moan that escaped her. Desire. Passion. She'd never experienced or been on the receiving end of either.

Justin's hand slid from her hip to her back and slipped under her blouse. The warmth of his hand on her skin sent a riotous wave of sensations through her. Willow clutched his arms and lifted her body closer to his. She wanted—needed—to get closer.

His mouth left hers, and his hands grasped her hips, stopping her from pressing against him. Her eyes drifted open at the loss of his lips.

He dropped his hands from her and rubbed them over his face. "That shouldn't have happened."

FOURTEEN

Justin stepped away from her before he was tempted to grab her again. He let out a rough sigh and willed his aroused body back into submission. Willow was innocent. She'd not only been sheltered her whole life, she'd also been kept prisoner by her insane family. She likely had no experience with men. And there he was trying to seduce her.

He stared at the ground and pictured an icy shower. When that didn't work, he switched to the time he'd gotten the brilliant idea to swim in an Alaskan lake. The icy water had practically turned him blue.

"Why shouldn't it have happened?"

Her soft voice drew his gaze.

She twisted her necklace around her finger and shifted from one foot to the other. "If you're not interested, then why did you kiss me? If it's because I'm helping you train, then I don't see how one has to affect the other. Or is it that you changed your mind after kissing me?"

"What?" Justin shook his head. "Trust me, sweetheart, I can't get much more interested than I am. We'd both be embarrassed if I did."

Willow's gaze dropped to the front of his jeans, and her eyes widened.

Yeah, so much for willing away my erection or protecting her innocence. He rubbed the back of his neck and huffed a laugh. "Stopping had nothing to do with lack of desire or with the fact that you're teaching me to control my magic."

She folded her arms over her waist. "Then I don't understand."

Justin sighed. He had no experience with this. *How am I supposed to explain my reticence to someone so innocent?*

The women he'd gotten involved with in the past had been far from innocent. Hell, the first woman he'd had sex with had been ten years older and decades more experienced. He only went for women looking for the same thing he was—a temporary release. He didn't do relationships.

"I don't want to take advantage of you."

"In what way does kissing me take advantage of me?" Willow scowled. "We're in the twenty-first century, Justin. Women can go out without a chaperone. They can even kiss a man who they're not married to."

He held up his hands. *Great, now she's getting pissed.* "I just don't want to give you the wrong idea."

Her eyes widened dramatically, and she batted her eyelashes at him. "You mean you aren't going to propose now that your lips have touched mine?"

Justin hunched his shoulders and sighed. *How had this gone so wrong?* "Between what you and Sebastian have revealed about your past, I got the impression that you've led a sheltered life. I'm trying to do the right thing here." He planted his fists on his hips.

Willow blushed and dropped her gaze.

Shit. Now he'd embarrassed her.

"In every way that matters, I'm a virgin. Before you, I'd never been kissed." She lifted her chin and met his gaze head on. "That doesn't mean I'm naïve or completely ignorant of how the world works. I've read—a lot. What else do you think I did with all that time on my hands?" Her cheeks were still bright pink. She slid the sea turtle on her necklace back and forth.

He'd thought she must be untouched, but hearing it from her lips left him undone. He'd been the first to kiss her.

"In case it wasn't obvious, I liked it when you kissed me. I'd really like to do it again sometime. Unless you really don't want to. You don't have to make up excuses. You also don't have to worry about taking advantage of me or giving me the wrong idea. I've read a lot of romance books. You're the classic commitment-phobic hero. I know full well anything between us would be temporary, and I'm okay with that."

Commitment-phobic hero? He would hardly describe himself as such. His lifestyle had never allowed for a relationship. He'd always moved from place to place. He wasn't afraid of a relationship, at least not in the way she meant. *How would I ever explain I'm a witch to a woman? Or what happened when I lost control of my powers? Or put her in danger because those who hunted me found me?*

Being that Willow was a witch and aware of all that made it a different situation. He didn't have to keep secrets from her. She wasn't helpless against his magic either. But she was still innocent. She should find a nice, normal guy for her first relationship.

He grimaced at the thought of another man touching her and being her first. He could be gentle with her. Another guy might not be.

"Did your front door do something to offend you, or are you figuring out a way to hide inside and forget this conversation ever happened?"

Justin frowned and glanced at Willow. "What?"

"You're scowling at your front door like you want to murder it or something."

He did his best to relax his face. "No, it just occurred to me you made a few good points."

"Just a few?"

He chuckled. "More than a few. Happy?"

"I will be when you elaborate on which of my excellent, insightful points you're referring to."

He laughed. "Let's see, the one where you're a grown woman capable of making her own decisions comes to mind."

"That is true and a perfect way to start. Continue."

Justin stepped forward and clasped her hips. He loved how she fit in his hands. "That I really like kissing you, too, and don't want to stop."

She slid her hands up over his shoulders as a smile spread across her face. "This is getting better and better. Anything else?"

"Just this." He lowered his head and captured her upturned mouth.

He had to remind himself to be gentle and take it slow repeatedly as need spiraled through his body at the way she fit in his arms and clutched his shoulders. Erotic little moans escaped from her.

Justin rested his forehead against hers. "I think we better see about that training before this gets out of hand."

FIFTEEN

Her phone rang, and Willow glanced at her purse on the passenger seat. *Why isn't it connected to the car?* She bit her lip and glanced down at the steering wheel. Sebastian had shown her how to operate her phone through the car more than once while lecturing her and making her promise not to talk or text while driving. She must've forgotten to link her phone again. Sebastian made her delete it each day for security reasons in case they had to ditch the car.

She grabbed her purse, dropped it on her lap, and stuck her hand in to dig around for her phone while keeping her gaze firmly on the road. Her fingers brushed against the smooth texture of her phone. She yanked it out. Cory was calling.

Willow swiped across the bottom to answer and tucked it between her shoulder and ear. "Hi, Cory."

"Hi. What are you up to? I thought I'd check in and see how everything is going."

"Good. I'm on my way to train with Justin. How are you and Finn doing? Still enjoying the road trip?"

"Yes, we spent a few days at the Grand Canyon. Have you ever been?"

Willow transferred her purse to the passenger seat and fumbled to put her phone on speaker. Her purse tipped off the seat. She lunged for it, dropped her phone, and swerved the car off the road.

The car rattled, and the sound of gravel crunched beneath the tires.

"Fiddlesticks!" Willow yanked the wheel back to the left.

"Willow? Are you okay? What's happening?" Cory's muffled voice came from the face down phone on the seat.

Willow flipped the phone over and glanced at the contents of her purse spilled across the floor. *This is why Sebastian lectured me about not driving and using my phone.*

"I'm fine. I'm not adept at multitasking while driving, apparently. The stupid phone didn't connect to the car. I didn't want to miss your call, and I ended up spilling my purse and dropping my phone. Can you hear me all right?"

Cory laughed. "I can hear you."

"Please don't mention this minor incident to Sebastian."

"I won't but on one condition. You have to tell me what the heck are fiddlesticks."

Willow grinned. "You know, I'm not really sure. I think it has something to do with a fiddle. I just always use the term when something goes wrong."

"Hmm... I suppose it's better than the expletives I let loose."

"Swearing was not allowed in my father's household. You forget he's centuries old and from a time when women weren't permitted to do many things modern-day women may take for granted."

"I can't imagine what growing up with that man—or thing, really—for a father was like for you."

"It wasn't pleasant. But in answer to your question, no, I've never been to the Grand Canyon. Is it as spectacular as pictures show?"

"Better, I think. It felt spiritual. I highly recommend putting it on your bucket list."

Willow frowned. She'd never made a bucket list. She'd never thought she would have the freedom to do things on any list she made—or the future to do them. "Do you have a bucket list?"

"I think I made one when I was a teenager. But I've got a blurry one in my head of places I'd like to see someday. You?"

"No. I mean, I guess I had dreams when I was younger of things I would do if I ever got free, but I think I stopped dreaming years ago."

"Maybe it's time you started again. You're free, Willow. I know we still have the threat of your family hanging over us, but we can't stop living. You should make a list."

"I might." *What would I put on it?* She would like to travel, she supposed. It would be nice to see some of the places she'd only read about.

"Speaking of dreams and things to put on a list of what you want to do, how are things going with Justin?"

Willow smiled. Justin did figure prominently in her dreams. And she would like to do plenty of things with him that she could put on the list. One of which would be to take their relationship beyond the kissing stage. It had been a week since their first kiss, and while he kissed her thoroughly every single day, he always stopped before it went further.

"As far as training goes, I'm not sure I can help him much more. He's gotten better at controlling his magic. He doesn't care for spell work, so we've been exploring his unique power and what he can use it for if it comes down to a battle."

"And have there been any developments of a more personal nature?"

Willow glanced at the phone.

Cory sighed. "I'm not-so-subtly trying to ask if you've acted on your attraction to him."

Willow chuckled. "Yeah, Cory, I know what you meant. I'm just thinking about what to say."

"So, there is something to say?"

"Yes. I mean, we've kissed—a lot. We flirt a lot. But he hasn't tried for more. Actually, he puts a stop to it any time we do get carried away."

"And you want more?"

"As you said, we need to live while we can. I don't want to wait." She didn't want to think about going into battle with her family and possibly losing her life before she ever had a chance to truly know a man's touch. To know Justin's touch.

"Does he know you've never been with anyone before? Because it might be hard to talk about, but I think it's important he knows."

"He knows."

"Good. If he's a good guy, he's probably trying to take things slow."

"So, how do I speed things along?" She didn't want to just blurt it out to him, but with her rising level of frustration, she might have to.

Cory laughed. "He's a guy, Willow. Guys are pretty much led by a certain piece of their anatomy. At least all the guys I've ever known. Seduce him."

Can I do that? She understood the concept but not the actual execution. Willow twisted her lips. "How do you suggest I go about that?"

"Every guy is a little different. Finn is a leg guy. He has a hard time keeping his eyes off mine. Where does Justin's gaze linger? Is he a breast guy? Show some cleavage. Ass guy? Find reasons to bend over." Cory chuckled. "If none of those work the way you want them to, stroke his package. Unless something else is going on, I'm quite sure that move is foolproof."

Heat flooded Willow's cheeks. *Could I be so bold?*

She made the turn onto Justin's road. She would have to consider it and make a plan. Glancing down at her khaki shorts and peach-colored blouse, she added *buy sexier clothes* to the imaginary list.

She huffed a breath. "I wish you were here. I could use your advice and suggestions. And maybe go shopping with you to help me pick out clothes that are less functional and more... revealing." She'd never once thought about buying clothes for anything but comfort or if she liked the way they looked or felt against her skin. Leaving behind her wardrobe when she'd left with Sebastian hadn't been a hardship. Her clothes had been tasteful but sedated.

"I've been thinking it might be time for us to join you. How else will we learn to fight together?"

"You're right. When do you think you'll be here?"

"Not sure yet. I have to talk Finn into it."

Willow laughed.

"He'd much rather keep me far from danger, but he'll have to see we're stronger together."

"If I thought running was the answer, I'd tell you to get as far away as you can. I think Sebastian has finally begun to agree that hiding will only work for so long."

"You keep working on your brother, and I'll work my wiles on Finn. Keep me posted on your progress with Justin too. I can't wait to hear how quickly he falls for whatever you've got planned for him."

Willow smiled as she parked the car and Justin walked off the path. "Bye, and good luck."

"You too."

The phone disconnected as Justin opened the door. He took her hand and pulled her out of the car and straight into his arms for a mind-melting kiss.

"Well, hello there." That was some greeting.

"Hi." He entwined their fingers and glanced into the car. "Do you need to grab...?" He frowned.

Willow looked over her shoulder. "Oh, I had a slight mishap and dumped my purse on the floor. Let me just grab my phone and keys."

Justin took her hand once again after she gathered her things and locked the car. She smiled as they walked down the path. Cory was right, she needed to take this seduction into her own hands. She glanced down. She would buy some lingerie with some new clothes. Something that made her feel sexy and confident enough to entice Justin.

CHAPTER

SIXTEEN

Willow swirled the surf in a circular pattern with her toes. Nerves had her shoulders stretched taut. She squirmed for a comfortable spot against the rock where she perched. Perhaps the beach wasn't a good spot for her and Justin to meet.

Since Sebastian had taken the car for the day, she'd thought it might be the opportune time to put her seduction plan into action. Justin had offered to pick her up, but she'd convinced him that practicing in a different terrain would be beneficial. She hadn't lied. Training against the other elements would help develop his fighting skills. Water was her and Sebastian's element, and though neither of them would be fighting Justin, the open ocean was also beneficial to air types like Miles because he had space to call the wind and storms.

Water normally calmed her, but anxiety was making her nauseous. She'd bought a bikini thinking it would make her sexier. The sky-blue set was mostly hidden beneath her see-through white top and white shorts. The weather was warm enough to wear just the swimsuit with the midday sun shining overhead, but her plan was for the hints of the suit underneath to grab his interest and provide a little mystery. Then, as they trained, she would gradually strip down to just the bikini.

Will that make me look desperate, though? What if I don't have the experience to pull it off without looking foolish?

Her toe brushed against something smooth in the sand beneath the water. She brushed against the object again and revealed a piece of green sea glass. Willow slid off the rock and picked it up. After brushing off the clinging sand and rinsing it in the surf, she held it up to the sunlight. Instead of the usual dark green, the piece was paler, like the leaves of the sage plants growing alongside their rental home. She slipped the piece into her pocket. Perhaps it would give her some luck.

Willow glanced up the empty beach to the path from the parking lot. Justin should arrive soon. Hopefully, the beach would remain empty. She'd only seen a handful of people use the beach the entire time they'd rented the house across the street. Sebastian had chosen it for its remoteness and its proximity to the water.

Should I lean against the rock or maybe recline slightly on top with my knee bent and my legs on display? Which would Justin find sexier? She put her hands on her hips and studied the rock.

"Hey."

She jumped and twirled. Her feet tangled together, and she toppled to the side.

Justin caught her and chuckled. "Sorry, I didn't mean to scare you."

Willow clutched his forearms and closed her eyes with a sigh. *How could I be so oblivious? Now, instead of looking sexy, I look clumsy and inept.*

"What were you staring at?"

"Hmm?" She blinked up at him.

He nodded toward the rock. "You looked like you were concentrating pretty hard."

"Oh, umm... nothing." *Great, now I look empty-headed too.* Willow dropped her forehead against his chest and groaned. Her plan was sunk before it had even started. It was probably for the best. The entire scheme consisted of ridiculous clichés. *What made me believe that sexy clothes and poses would suddenly make him desperate for me?*

"Willow, what's wrong?" Justin pulled her into a hug and rubbed her back.

She wrapped her arms around his waist and cuddled against his chest. "Nothing."

"Does nothing mean the same as fine in woman language?"

She lifted her head and frowned.

His eyebrows pinched together. "Even I know that if a woman says she's fine, she's actually the exact opposite."

Willow smiled. "I had a stupid idea. Let's just call it momentary insanity and forget it ever happened, okay?"

He joined his hands at the small of her back and kissed her forehead. "Tell me."

She shook her head and buried it under his chin. "Please drop it. It's too embarrassing."

"That just makes me want to know even more." He chuckled.

"Ugh, fine, I had this stupid plan to seduce you, okay?"

"Willow..."

"Please, can we just drop it?"

"Look at me."

"No."

Justin lifted her chin.

She reluctantly dragged her gaze up the navy-blue T-shirt spanning his chest, over the stubble peppering his chin, past his full lips, to his warm brown eyes.

"You seduce me just by breathing."

Her core clenched and heated.

He lowered his head, and his warm breath caressed her skin. "I don't want to rush you or push you into anything you're not ready for." His lips brushed hers in a featherlight kiss.

"You're not." She pressed her lips against his. "I don't want to wait."

Their tongues tangled in a deep kiss. His thumb traced her jawline, and his hand clasped her neck. Willow's fingers delved into his soft hair at the back of his neck as desire left a trail of warmth spiraling through her.

Justin separated their lips with a gasp and pressed her head against his chest. "I want you to be sure."

"I am."

"Then tomorrow. After training."

"Why not now?" She tilted her head up. "Why do we have to wait? Our rental is right across the street."

He smiled and tucked her hair behind her ear. "Because, for one, I want to cook you dinner. I want to give you a proper date at least. And two, I didn't come prepared. I want to protect you."

"Protect me from what?"

Justin chuckled. "I don't have any condoms."

Scorching heat spread over her face and chest. *Willow, you're an idiot.* "Of course. I should've thought of that."

"That's my job." He planted a soft kiss on her lips. "It's your first time. I want to make it as special as I can."

He was being sweet and considerate.

She sighed and looped her arms loosely over his shoulders. "I suppose you want to actually train, then, today?"

Justin threw his head back and laughed.

She resisted the urge to trace her tongue over his Adam's apple and tan throat. Frustrated desire still heated her skin. Perhaps she should take a quick swim in the cold Pacific to cool off.

Justin kissed her shoulder over the exposed strap of her bikini. Her shirt had shifted off it during their kiss.

"How about we sit and talk for a while instead? Training can wait." He gently pulled her down onto the beach to sit between his legs with her back against his chest.

Willow snuggled against him, staring out at the ocean. A large container ship sailed on the horizon. Waves lapped at the shore. Her toes dug into the soft sand. The warmth from Justin's body surrounded her.

She tilted her head back to rest on his shoulder. The day might be salvageable after all. Already, it might be in the top ten of her best days.

"What are you thinking about?"

"That this moment right here is pretty perfect, and I want to imprint it on my memory."

He kissed the side of her neck. "It is pretty perfect."

"Cory gave me the idea of making a bucket list of all the things I want to do and experience. I wasn't sure what to put on it other than traveling. But what I really want is more moments like this one."

"I've traveled the world for work, but I concentrated on the job. I didn't sightsee much. This is better." His arms circled her waist.

She rested her hands on top of his. "Do you enjoy your job? I confess I don't know much about mining."

He gave a slight shrug. "I'm good at it. My magic guides me to find what's hidden from most. Modern technology only shows us so much. What lies beneath the ground is still pretty much a mystery. Digging test holes involves a lot of educated guessing. My success rate is better than most."

"Sometimes, I wonder what profession I would've chosen if my life had been different. I've never held an actual job."

"What do you think you would choose?"

"I'm not sure. I'd like to help people, but I'm not a healer. I thought maybe a teacher. I like kids. They're kinder than adults. They haven't been jaded by life yet."

"I can see you as a teacher. You've taught me."

Willow smiled at him. It was probably silly to dream about what could've been or what might be, but even having the hope of options was so new. "I don't know what the future holds, but I want to live. I want to enjoy every moment." Her smile dimmed. She used to believe her death was imminent, and maybe it still was, but that was even more reason to revel in days like that one.

Justin nuzzled the side of her head and kissed her cheek. "I've spent most of my life running. Enjoying the moment was the farthest thing from my mind."

"When you're just trying to survive, it's hard to stop and smell the roses."

"Survival was part of it. I was taught to stay hidden. I ran from anyone who might find out about my powers. We ended up having to leave because I lost control. By the time I became an adult, it was already ingrained to keep moving and keep my distance from anyone." His thumb stroked her wrist. "I've been running from the guilt too. When you're constantly on the move, your thoughts don't have a chance to grab hold and drag you into the past as much."

"Guilt about what? Losing control of your powers?"

"My mother."

Willow shifted so she could see his face clearer. "Your mother wasn't your fault. My father was the one most likely responsible."

"But he wouldn't have had a chance to find her if not for me."

"I don't understand."

"We never stayed in one place long. I told you that. We'd already been here longer than she liked. She wanted to leave—had already packed our stuff. But I wanted to go to this birthday party. It was at a laser tag place with an arcade. It was pretty much all I could think about. So I begged and cajoled her. I promised her everything I could think of, and she gave in. If we'd left when she wanted, she'd be alive."

"Justin, no. You can't blame yourself. There's no way you could've known, and you were a child."

He turned his gaze from the ocean to her. "I knew."

"How?"

"I'd gone on a field trip the week before. I'd lost control and caused a landslide. I didn't tell her. I knew if I did, we'd be gone in an instant."

"You don't know if that's why you were found." She searched her memory. *Had anyone in my family mentioned a landslide or finding a witch with earth power back then?* It was so long ago. "Besides, you aren't to blame regardless. The one who killed her is." *My father. It had to be.* "I don't know how you can stand to be near me knowing it was probably my father who killed your mother. I come from evil—pure evil." Willow sat up. She was tainted.

"You're not your family." He pulled her back into his arms and tucked her head under his chin. "Why are we ruining our day talking about the past?"

Willow sighed and relaxed against him. He was right. Their pasts shouldn't mar their perfect day.

A tingle of recognition wiggled up her spine.

"What the hell is this?"

CHAPTER

SEVENTEEN

Willow scrambled to her feet as Sebastian stalked toward them, murder in his eyes. *What is he doing here? He's supposed to be gone until late tonight!* "Sebastian—"

A blast of power whipped past her. She turned in horror toward Justin. Sebastian was out for blood. Justin stood behind her with his hands up and a scowl on his face.

He managed to block Sebastian's magic. Willow jumped in front of Justin to protect him from her brother and prevent Justin from retaliating until she could calm Sebastian down and talk some sense into him.

"Willow," Sebastian growled.

Justin put his hands on her arms and lifted her out of the way. "Stay out of the way, sweetheart."

She ran to Sebastian and grabbed his hands. "Stop!"

Sebastian yanked his hands from her grasp and pointed at Justin. "I warned you. I told you what I would do if you harmed my sister."

"He hasn't hurt me!"

Sebastian scowled at her. "He had his hands on you."

"I wanted his hands on me."

Her brother's eyes widened then narrowed. He shoved her behind him. Before she could react, a burst of power energized the air. A wave of water rose out of the ocean.

"No!" she screamed. Justin would be washed out to sea. Willow pushed past Sebastian.

Justin no longer stood where she'd last seen him. A tower of rock stood in his place. The wave crashed against the rock.

Her gaze rose to the top of the towering mass. Justin stood there, staring down at Sebastian and her. "Move, Willow."

He used his powers to build a tower of rock out of the ground. Willow closed her gaping mouth with a snap. She would think more about the awesomeness of that later. She threw herself at Sebastian before he could attempt anything else. "Please don't hurt him!" She wrapped her arms tightly around his neck. "If you care for me at all..."

Sebastian sighed and hugged her. "You're the only one in this world I care about."

"Then stop and listen to me."

The ground vibrated beneath her feet. She glanced over her shoulder. Justin stalked toward them.

Willow held up a hand. "Let me talk to my brother alone, please."

Justin glared at Sebastian over her head. "If you harm one hair on her head..."

Sebastian tensed against her.

"He won't. He wouldn't." Willow pleaded with Justin with her eyes. She needed to talk to her brother alone to get him to see reason.

Justin's expression softened as he stared at her, and he nodded. "I'll be waiting for your call."

Sebastian tensed again. She absently patted his shoulder while sending Justin a small smile and nod.

Willow kept her body between Sebastian and Justin as he walked across the beach and up the path. Once he was out of sight, she whirled back to her brother.

"You can't trust him, Willy."

Her shoulders drooped. "Basty, aren't you tired of not trusting anyone? I am."

"I trust you."

"Then trust me to make my own decisions. I'm an adult. You can't keep protecting me from everything in life. I love you for it, but I have to choose for myself."

Sebastian scowled and stared out at the sea. "You've never had a relationship with a man. They don't think like women. He's after one thing."

"You're a man. Are you saying that's all you're ever after with a woman?"

His gaze swerved to her. "That's exactly what I'm saying."

Willow sighed. "I hope one day you meet a woman that you do want more with." She wrapped her arms around her waist. "I've never even had *that*. Is it so wrong for me to want a man to desire me? To know what it feels like to have a man kiss me, hold me, or make love to me?"

Sebastian grimaced. "And when he hurts you?"

"Then he hurts me. At least I'll be living instead of just existing. He's been very forthcoming that he's not a relationship type. In fact, I was the one who pursued him. How do you know I won't be the one who hurts him? I'm not a fragile doll, Basty."

He jerked his chin toward her necklace. "I can't help but think our mother believed she knew what she was doing when she got involved with Edward. And it killed her. I can't lose you too."

Tears filled Willow's eyes. "Justin isn't like our father. Don't compare the two."

"You've known him for a few weeks. You have no idea what he's like."

Willow shook her head. "That's not true."

"Anyone can put on the charm for a short while—even Edward is capable when he wants something enough. Our mother probably said the same things you're saying now."

Willow squeezed her eyes shut. Sebastian had always put their mother on a pedestal, like she was some kind of saint their father had destroyed. He'd turned her into a martyr. Willow had thought she'd been protecting her brother by keeping secrets, but she'd been wrong. "She knew. She knew what he was—what he wanted. She made that choice."

"What the hell are you talking about? He killed her. He sacrificed her to extend his own miserable life. Do you really think she would've chosen death over staying with us and raising us? Do you ever wonder what our lives could've been if he hadn't killed her?"

Willow placed her hand on his arm. "Basty, she's not dead. He took her power, but she survived. She made a deal with him. She gave him her power in exchange for money. She never wanted us. She chose to leave us with a man she knew was a monster."

EIGHTEEN

Sebastian jerked away from Willow. He stared at her like she was a stranger. A stranger he wanted to hurt.

Willow raised her hands to plead with him to understand. "I had a vision when we were twelve. I saw her negotiating with him. I saw the whole thing. I didn't want to believe it, so I snuck into his office and did some digging. He paid for an exclusive long-term care facility—for her. She's in a wheelchair and needs care, but she survived with all her mental faculties in place. I looked the place up. It's like a spa for wealthy residents."

"If any of that is true, why would he let us believe she was dead? Why would he let us think he'd killed her? He would've held her well-being over our heads just like he uses ours against each other." Fury dripped from his words and lined his face.

"It was part of their deal. She signed away all rights to us. She sold us to him, Basty. She never cared for us. We were her currency to a carefree life." Stacia, Miles and Miranda's mother, was more of a mother to them than theirs had ever been.

He shook his head. "Why would you keep this from me?"

"To protect you. You had her on a pedestal. I didn't want to destroy your image of her like mine was destroyed. It devastated me."

He stared at her coldly—like she was nothing to him. "What other secrets are you keeping from me?"

She frantically shook her head. "None. Just that one."

"I guess I can't trust anyone—not even you. You're just like everyone else." Sebastian stalked away.

Willow latched onto his arm. "Sebastian, please. I was trying to protect you."

He shrugged off her hold. "I can't even look at you right now." Sebastian strode away.

Willow crumpled to the ground and sobbed. *He'll never forgive me.* She'd lost the one person always in her corner. The one person she thought would always love her unconditionally.

Footsteps approached.

Willow yanked her head up. *Did he come back? Will he listen to my explanation?*

Justin dropped to his knees beside her. "What happened? Are you hurt?" He scanned her body.

She shook her head and threw herself into his arms.

He pulled her onto his lap as he sat on the beach. "What is it?"

"He hates me. He's so angry."

"Because of us? That's unreasonable, Willow. But..." He sighed and hugged her close. "What do you want to do? If you want to end this—"

She vehemently shook her head. "It's not us." She couldn't bear to lose Justin, too, not then.

"Then what is it?"

Willow scrubbed her cheeks and choked back her sobs. "What are you doing here? How did you know?"

"I didn't feel right leaving you like that, so I parked up the street to make sure you were okay. Then I saw your brother stalk to the house and take off in the car. I came down to check on you."

"Thank you." She leaned against his shoulder as her body shuddered with the remainder of her tears.

"Talk to me, Willow." Justin rubbed her back.

"I told him a secret I've been keeping from him."

"Do you want to tell me what it is? If you don't, that's okay."

"I thought I was protecting him. I thought I was doing the right thing. But now I see that he'll never forgive me for it. I betrayed him. I've lost my brother."

"Your brother loves you. He's an asshole, but it's clear he cares for you. He'll come around. Let him cool off."

Willow shook her head. "You don't understand. I let him think our mother was dead, and she's not."

Justin stiffened against her.

She lifted her head. "See, even you think it's terrible."

"I'm sure you had your reasons."

She nodded. "I did. Sebastian always put her on a pedestal. In his eyes, she died to save us."

"It was a lie?"

"She made a deal with our father. She signed away all rights to us. She willingly let him take her powers. All for money. She didn't want us."

Justin tucked her under his chin. "I'm sorry, Willow. Did you tell your brother that?"

"Yes. But all he cares about is that I kept it from him."

"Give him time. He'll see why you did it."

"Would you forgive me? If I had kept that secret from you?"

Justin sighed.

"You wouldn't."

"I didn't say that."

"It's written all over your face."

She sat up and tried to pull away, but he held her close.

"Hold on. I would probably react in anger like he did. I'd be pissed off, but that doesn't mean I would never forgive you. Secrets don't end well when they come out. Someone will always get hurt. Your heart was in the right place, but I can see why he's upset."

A sob strangled her throat and twisted her lips.

"Shh, it'll be okay." Justin held her while she cried. "It'll take him a while to reconcile the truth with the past he believed was real. If I found out my mother was alive..." He shook his head. "It's hard to fathom. I don't even know if my father is alive or dead. He didn't want me, so I didn't want him. Sebastian always believed his mother wanted him, that she sacrificed herself for him, that she was taken from him."

Justin's mouth continued to move, but she couldn't hear the words. Her sight blurred along the edges and cold seeped over her skin. *A vision.* Darkness shrouded the beach, and the scenery faded. Her senses dulled. She couldn't hear Justin or the ocean's surf. She couldn't feel his arms around her. Even the salty taste of the air evaporated.

Sound returned first. But not sound from where she was. The sound came from whatever the vision would show her. Children laughed. A dog barked. A murmur of voices. A sizzling sound. Black turned gray, and a scene came into focus. Several people milled among picnic tables. There were trees, a pond. Children played with a dog and a frisbee.

A park. A picnic?

A man stood in front of a grill filled with hamburgers and hot dogs. He smiled as he glanced at the children playing. Willow gasped. His features were almost identical to Justin's but older, and he didn't have Justin's wide shoulders. A young woman approached him with a smile that turned into a frown as she appeared to stare straight at Willow.

The man smiled at the woman. "Burgers and hot dogs are almost done." His smile dimmed at her continued frown. "What is it?" He looked over his shoulder.

"There's a presence, Dad. Someone is watching us."

"A witch?"

She nodded and peered closer.

The man searched the area with his gaze. "I sense nothing. Are you sure? Should I sound the alarm? Do you sense danger?"

She shook her head. "No, but I still don't like it." She raised her hands and whispered a spell.

Birds dove through the air straight at Willow. She screamed and jerked back.

A roaring filled her ears. Her vision faded to bright white. Hands shook her shoulders. Justin's concerned face hovered above her. His lips moved, but she couldn't hear him.

She gasped as sound returned.

He was shouting her name. "Willow!"

"I'm... I'm okay."

"Jesus, what is it? Should I take you to the hospital? Are you sick? You were as white as a sheet and unresponsive. It was like you were staring straight through me." He yanked her into his arms and stood. "I'm taking you to the hospital."

"No."

"Willow..."

"It was a vision. I'm fine. I just need water. Preferably to drink, but since we don't have any, just put me in the ocean." Weakness weighed down her limbs and made her brain sluggish. The water would revive her.

Justin looked at the ocean then up the path. He grimaced and walked to the water.

She thought he would put her down, but instead, he walked right into the surf until she floated in his arms. The connection to her element instantly soothed her. Her extremities tingled as the water restored her power. She sighed and let her eyes drift closed.

"Willow?"

She forced a smile and opened her eyes. Justin stared down at her, a concerned look etched on his face.

"I'm okay." She glanced around them. "We can get out. You didn't have to come in with me. Your clothes are soaked."

"I'm fine. Is it helping? You're not as pale."

"Yes. I'm much better."

Justin nodded and carried her out of the water.

"I want to take you back to my place, but yours is closer." He looked up the path with a frown.

"I could use a drink of water and dry clothes. Why don't we go across the street? I don't think Sebastian's clothes will fit you, but I can at least give you a towel or two to dry off."

He started across the beach with her still in his arms.

"Justin, I can walk. Put me down."

"Regain your strength. You weigh next to nothing." He continued to trudge across the sand.

"The water revived me. I feel better, really."

"Good." He still didn't put her down.

She clutched his shoulders and peered at the path as it turned from sand to rock and dirt. Once they reached the top, he carried her across the road and up the driveway to the house.

How will I explain my vision to him?

He set her down at the front door, and she opened it.

"Justin, I have to tell you about my vision."

He glanced at her as he followed her inside. "After you drink some water and get into dry clothes."

"But it concerns you. Justin, I think I saw your father. He looked just like you. You said your mother told you he was normal. But he's a witch, and I think you have a sister who's a witch too."

CHAPTER
NINETEEN

Justin froze. He stared down at Willow's pale hand clutching his wrist. *Why would she have a vision of someone she thought was my father? It didn't make sense. His father wasn't a witch. She must be mistaken.*

He lifted his gaze and forced a small smile. "You should go change." He glanced around the square space. The living room had a couch facing the window to take advantage of the ocean view. An archway to the left led to a kitchen. "I'll get you some water while you put on dry clothes."

"Justin, did you hear what I said?"

"I heard you. We'll talk after." He gave her a slight push toward the short hallway at the back of the room, which he assumed led to their bedrooms.

After giving him a confused look, Willow walked to an open doorway on the right at the back of the house. He went into the kitchen and opened the cabinets until he found a glass and poured her water.

He leaned with his hands on the counter and stared out the window over the sink at the ocean. Her vision must have been of someone that resembled him. *How could she possibly know for sure it's my father? Even I don't know what my father looks like. Or maybe it was from the past. Though his mother had never mentioned his father having another family. She hadn't said much about him at all beyond the fact that he hadn't wanted them.*

"I brought you a towel." Willow stood behind him holding out a white towel. She'd changed into pants and a sweatshirt. She rubbed another towel over her wet hair.

"Thanks." He handed her the glass of water and took the towel.

"I could throw your clothes in the washer then dryer. The salt water must make them uncomfortable." She frowned as her gaze wandered over him. "I really don't think Sebastian has any clothes that would fit you, but I'll go check."

She disappeared before he could tell her not to bother. A little discomfort wouldn't kill him. He was used to a lot worse than wearing wet clothes. He'd worked while covered in mud, dirt, rock, and a host of other materials over the years. He used the towel to dry his hair and exposed skin.

Willow appeared holding out a pair of black shorts. "These might fit. They're loose, and they stretch." She lifted a black tank top from underneath the shorts. "And I thought you could give this a try. You're taller and broader than Sebastian, but they're better than wet clothes."

He nodded and took the clothes from her. "Appreciate it."

"The bathroom's on the left."

White tiles covered the floor and small bathroom's walls. Interspersed among the white, sailboats and sea creatures decorated colorful tiles. He put the clean clothes on the edge of the pedestal sink while he dragged off his wet T-shirt and jeans. He doubted her brother would be too happy when he found out Justin wore his clothes. Though the man never seemed particularly happy about anything.

Willow waited for him in the living room, drinking another glass of water. She gave him a small smile. "Not bad."

He glanced down at the shorts and tank top that were a size too small. "They're fine. Thanks."

"Can we talk about my vision now?"

Justin nodded, and she sat in the corner of the couch with her legs drawn up and her arms wrapped around them.

He sat next to her. "What makes you so sure it was my father?"

"At first, I thought it might be you, only older. But then I realized there were differences. He's not as tall or muscular as you. His hair isn't as dark. You have the same eyes, though. So does the woman who called him Dad."

"Still doesn't make it my father. Let's say it is, though. It could've been the past, right? You said you have visions of both the past and the future."

"Yes. The present, too, sometimes. It's not always easy to pinpoint the exact date, but I have a knowing sense, and I've learned to note the details of a vision so I can decipher it. For instance, the woman was wearing a smart watch. Music played off to the right somewhere. I don't know the name of the song or who sings it, but I've heard it on the radio recently. I know it's a current hit. It definitely wasn't the past. It's possible it was the future, but my instincts tell me it was the present."

"What makes you think he's a witch?"

"I saw their power auras. They're both witches. She sensed me, too, and used magic. I think she might control animals. She said a spell, and birds flew at me."

Justin folded his arms over his chest. *My mother wouldn't have lied to me. There must be some other explanation.* "How accurate are your visions? Are you ever wrong? Could you have unconsciously misinterpreted what you saw?"

Willow rested her chin on her knees. "They're never wrong. It's not like I'm looking at a blurry scene. It's like watching a show on television. Once the vision comes into focus, I see and hear everything crystal clear. I don't always understand what I'm shown at the time, but I don't think I'm wrong about it being your father." She peered up at him. "What exactly did your mother tell you about him? Did she have pictures?"

He shook his head. "She had no pictures. They weren't together long. She said he didn't want a family. He knew about me. She didn't say it outright, but I heard her talking to my grandmother once. He had seen her do something magical and didn't handle it well. My mother and grandmother were arguing. We'd had to move again because I had broken all the windows in the house where we'd been staying when I lost control of my power. My grandmother had brought him up. I think she wanted my mother to ask him for help with me. Mom became irate. I'd never seen her yell at her mother before. She said she would never contact him or go begging for help. She said he made it clear he didn't want us and never would."

"I'm so sorry, Justin." Willow scooted over and took his hand. "I don't understand the discrepancy. I only know what I saw."

"You said the witch sensed you. Is that normal?"

"No, it's the first time, actually. Her aura was powerful, but I've had visions of powerful witches before, and they've never sensed me. I don't fully understand it. I was standing close to them. Maybe that had something to do with it. Or maybe it has something to do with her power."

"Are your visions always connected to the people you're with?"

"You mean did I have the vision of your father and sister because you were with me?"

Justin nodded.

"No. Edward used to test my powers. He wanted to prompt my visions. He would try different emotional states like fear and anger and had me touch people or items. None of it worked. I feel like my visions are meant to help me or show me a certain path."

How could a vision of a man who never wanted or knew me in any way help her? "In what way?"

"You're the only one outside my family that I've ever had more than one vision of."

"I wasn't in this vision."

"No, but it's connected to you. I wasn't really referring to this one, though. You know about the one I had of you causing the earthquake in Mexico and the one of you here, which led us to you. But I had one before those. I never told anyone about it." Willow twisted the charm on her necklace with her free hand. She seemed to do that whenever she was nervous.

"Do you have that necklace to remind you of the sea?"

She glanced down at the sea turtle between her fingers. "No. It was my mother's. I wear it to remind me of her betrayal. I know that probably seems dark. It was one of the few things she left behind. Sebastian found it and gave it to me to wear. This was before I knew what she'd done. When I learned of her betrayal, I smashed it with a rock. I hit it over and over again." She held it away from her neck and turned it over. "See the scratches and the two little dents?"

Justin held the charm and ran his thumb over the surface. It wasn't as smooth as it appeared. He nodded and dropped the necklace back against her chest.

"It didn't break. I almost threw it in the trash, but at the last second, I changed my mind. In that moment, I felt like the sea turtle —battered and thrown away. I put the necklace back on because it survived my attack and reminds me that I've survived too."

"You're a survivor."

Willow gave him a sad smile. "The first vision of you was when I was twenty-one. Sebastian had graduated college and was going to law school. I saw him less and less. You have to remember I wasn't allowed to leave the estate unsupervised. Sebastian had been my only friend." She plucked at the hem of her sweatshirt. "I was in a low place." She peeked at him before dropping her gaze to the floor. "A very dark place."

He intertwined their fingers and stroked her wrist with his thumb.

"I'd systematically stolen pain medication from our housekeeper over the past several months. She never noticed the one or two pills I took." Willow tensed. "I took them all and lay down on my bed."

Justin stiffened. Rage toward her tormentors filled him. *She tried to kill herself. Her pain was so deep that she wanted to end it all. I never would have met her. Her beautiful light would've been snuffed out before I ever had a chance to know her.* Justin scooped her into his arms and held her on his lap.

She rested her head on his shoulder. "That's when I had a vision of you. I don't know where you were. There was tall grass and a few trees. You stood on a rocky outcropping staring at a lake. You were so handsome and strong. I wanted to know everything about you. When I woke from the vision, I dashed into the bathroom and stuck my fingers down my throat to vomit up the pills. It was awful. I was so weak." Willow clasped her hands between her knees. "If I hadn't had that vision…"

He lifted her chin with his thumb and forefinger. "Promise me you'll never attempt anything like that again. Promise me you'll call me. No matter where I am, I'll find you." He didn't make the promise lightly. He didn't know what the future held for either of them, but he could make her that promise.

She gave him a tearful smile. "I promise."

Justin kissed her forehead and tucked her against his chest. He didn't understand her visions or why she'd had one of him that day. It could've been anywhere in the world. With that timeline, it might have been Africa. It didn't matter. If it stopped her from taking her life, he was glad. It might've been a coincidence, or it could've been something more. He certainly didn't comprehend magic or where it came from.

"I told you this because I want you to understand why I think my vision of your father and sister is important. It means something."

"Okay." If she needed it to mean something, he wouldn't argue.

"You were only a little kid when your mother died. Our perspectives and memories as children aren't always accurate. Or maybe your mother had her reasons for keeping secrets from you."

He stiffened.

Willow rushed on. "Or maybe your father kept the fact that he was a witch from her. We don't know. The point is, I think we need to find out. It can't be a coincidence that we're trying to form a coven and you have a family of witches somewhere that might help."

She wanted to locate his father and whatever family the man had formed without him and his mother. Willow was wrong. He didn't have a family somewhere. He might share blood with those people, but that didn't make them a family.

Willow leaned her forehead against the windowpane. The overcast sky matched her mood. It was gray, dreary, and damp outside with the occasional sprinkle mixed in. The guilt and sadness left her feeling the same way.

Sebastian wouldn't return her texts or calls. He hadn't been back to the house since he stormed away two days ago. A lot could happen in two days. *Where is he? What is he doing? Will he ever come back?*

Even Justin seemed to have deserted her after their conversation about her vision. He'd canceled their date and their training. He'd used the word postponed rather than canceled, so she was holding on to that. At least he returned her texts—eventually. He insisted everything was fine and that he had some things to take care of. What those things were, he didn't share.

Did I cross our casual line when I confessed my suicide attempt? Did that drive him away? Or was it my vision of his father and new family? She could understand him needing time to mull over the possibilities. *But couldn't we discuss them together? Is he freaked out that my first vision of him saved my life? That might've been too much too soon.*

She didn't regret sharing any of it with him. No more secrets. If it pushed him away, so be it. At least the guilt she'd been drowning in was gone. It was better to know that he couldn't handle that side of her. *It would've been nice to know his touch first.*

Willow glanced at her phone on the coffee table. The screen was as blank as the last few dozen times she'd checked. It had survived a dunk in the ocean, but it still felt like it was punishing her for the abuse with silence.

She was attributing a revenge plot to an inanimate object. She gently banged her forehead against the glass. She needed to get out of there and do something. Sebastian had the car, but she could figure out how to use one of those car services. *How hard could it be to download an app and request a car? I have fake identification and a credit card.*

Freedom was finally at her fingertips, and she couldn't think of a single place she wanted to go—except Justin's cabin. She couldn't just show up when he had asked for time. *He probably isn't even there.*

Willow walked to the couch and tucked herself into the corner. Perhaps she should try immersing herself in the bathtub again, like she had earlier in the hopes of initiating a vision. It'd never worked in the past, when her father had practically drowned her in his attempts to force a vision, but she'd thought that if she relaxed, it might bring a different result.

She'd wanted a vision to locate her brother and make sure he was safe. It hadn't worked. Her fingers were wrinkled, but they'd bounce back. She'd used all the hot water, but it should've had enough time to replenish by then. It was better than sitting there worrying and doing nothing. At least she would feel like she was trying to accomplish something. She stood and walked toward the bathroom.

The front door rattled.

Willow whirled as the door swung open, and Sebastian walked in. He spared her a glance while slamming the door and locking it.

"Sebastian…"

He held up a hand to silence her and strode into the kitchen.

She stood in the opening while he chugged a bottle of water from the fridge. *Why is he so thirsty? Did he deplete himself using magic?*

"What happened? Did they find you?" She stepped closer. *Did Miles or Miranda attack him?*

Sebastian tossed her a glare and threw the empty bottle into the recycling bin. He was still pissed.

She sighed. "Basty, I was worried about you. I *am* worried about you. I get that you're angry, but can you please answer me?"

He leaned with his back against the counter and folded his arms. "No, they didn't find me."

"Then what's with the water?" *He wouldn't have fought with Justin, would he?*

"I needed to let loose a bit." He shrugged one shoulder.

That sounded like him. He'd often used magic to release tension or anger.

"Will you ever forgive me?"

He stared at her silently.

"Haven't you kept secrets from me for my protection? Why is this so different?"

"It's not the same."

"Yes, it is. You've always felt like you needed to protect me. I was trying to do the same. I realize now that it wasn't the right choice, but I was a child. I didn't want to take away your hope, Basty. The knowledge devastated me, and I didn't want you to feel it too."

Sebastian turned his gaze to the window.

Maybe she should be grateful he returned at all. In time, he might understand and forgive her. *At least I know he's okay.* Willow turned to go. She placed a hand on the archway trim and glanced over her shoulder. "I love you. I'm glad you're back." She walked down the hall to her bedroom. She would give him space.

"I went to see her."

She froze then retraced her steps to the kitchen. He still leaned in the same spot, staring out the window.

He went to see our mother?

"She was where you said she was."

"Did you talk to her?"

"I planned to." He snorted. "She was laughing and playing cards like she didn't have a care in the world. I stood by the door less than ten feet from her. I had no idea what to say. I think I believed that she wouldn't really be there—that you were mistaken. I waited for her to look at me. I wanted to see if the happiness on her face would turn to joy or fade to fear or anger." He stuffed his hands in his pants pocket. "Her gaze drifted over to me and locked with mine for a moment. Then she turned back to her game and laughed at something one of the players said." Sebastian pinned Willow with his gaze. "She didn't recognize me. Or if she did, she didn't show it or care."

"Oh, Basty." Willow removed the distance between them and wrapped him in her arms.

He didn't pull away, but he didn't return her hug either.

"It's her loss, not yours."

He sighed and hugged her. "Don't ever lie to me again, Willy."

"I won't. As long as you promise the same to me."

His scruff scratched her neck as he nodded. "Promise."

"No more secrets." Willow rested her head on his shoulder. "And no more ignoring my messages or calls because you're angry. Just text me you're okay."

"Sorry."

The knot of worry in her stomach loosened. *I haven't lost my brother.*

"Why aren't you training with earthquake boy?"

Willow half laughed while she drew back to stare at Sebastian. "Earthquake boy? Please tell me you're not going to start calling him that."

"Fits, doesn't it?"

"So he should call you tsunami or rogue wave or something?"

Sebastian rolled his eyes. "Ha ha. You're deflecting. What's up?"

She explained her vision of Justin's father and family and the fact that they were witches. "He just needed to postpone training for a bit." She left out the part about her first vision of Justin and her suicide attempt. That wasn't something she ever wanted to share with her brother. He wouldn't understand.

Willow walked to the fridge and grabbed some berries to make a fruit salad. *It isn't lying not to tell him.* There must be plenty of things he didn't tell her, and she didn't expect him to—unless it involved her. Besides, her depression was in the past. If it became an issue again, then she would tell him. She'd managed to endure the last two days without spiraling out of control. That was progress. She hadn't once slipped into thoughts of harming herself.

She had hope. Hope that her life could be different. Hope that her life could have meaning. Hope that she didn't have to be perpetually alone.

CHAPTER
TWENTY-ONE

The water lapped at her chin. Willow lowered her arms from the sides of the bathtub and into the warm bath. She rested her head against the smooth, cool edges of the claw-foot tub.

Her emotions were no longer a riotous mess. Sebastian was back, and he'd forgiven her. Justin had called her about an hour ago to ask her to lunch the next day. She was calm. A little nervous about seeing Justin, but still calm. A perfect time to attempt to spur her visions.

A trio of candles flickered on the vanity opposite the tub. She was thankful Sebastian had insisted she take the primary bedroom with the attached bathroom when they moved into the rental. It gave her privacy for her attempt. Not that Sebastian was likely to disturb her. The past two days of travel had exhausted him, and he had crashed soon after taking a shower earlier that evening.

Willow closed her eyes and tried to empty her mind. She took deep cleansing breaths and recited the spell she'd written earlier. "Let me see. Release the key. Show me what I seek. Give me a peek."

She pictured Justin's father and sister as she'd seen them in her last vision and repeated the spell over and over. She needed their location. They were witches. She'd used her visions to locate witches before.

Her hands floated to the top of the water. The normal house sounds faded. The drip of the faucet stopped. The buzzing hum of the light fixture disappeared. Her mind drifted like it, too, would float away.

The water chilled. A horn blared, but it wasn't a car. It sounded like a boat horn from a ship. Cars driving by. City sounds. Her vision cleared.

A man sat in a chair on a deck surrounded by a thick fog bank. The horn blared again. A light flared, and a small puff of smoke rose. A sweet scent reached her. Justin's father smoked a cigar.

She cast her gaze away from him and searched the surroundings for clues to his location. Water. Water was nearby. Lots of houses and buildings. It was an urban area.

The horn blared, and she turned, then gasped. *Golden Gate Bridge.* Justin's father was in San Francisco.

"Papa!" A little boy ran across the deck and jumped on the man's lap.

"Arthur." A woman's chastising voice prompted him to hastily extinguish his cigar.

I have a name.

Several people entered the scene, greeting him with smiles, laughter, and affection. The family loved one another.

Her mind and body felt like they were being ripped away, as if she'd reached the end of a bungy cord. Darkness surrounded her as she plummeted and spun out of control. Nausea and confusion spiraled inside her.

Voices argued around her. She couldn't make out the words. Shapes solidified into people—familiar people, Miles and Miranda.

Wait, they're arguing about Cory. Do they know where she is?

"We'll catch up to them by tomorrow. We know where they're headed." Miranda tapped her fingers on her folded arms—a sure sign she was angry.

"All the more reason we leave tonight."

"The idiot is visiting his old soldier buddy. He's not going anywhere, and I'm tired." Miranda dropped onto a hotel bed.

Miles stormed from the room.

They know where Cory and Finn are! I have to warn them.

Miranda's sat up, and her eyes narrowed. "I feel you spying, little sister." Her gaze searched the room. "I'll have to teach you some manners." She stood, and her gaze landed on Willow. "I'll be seeing you real soon."

Willow propelled her mind back into her body. *Could Miranda read my mind in a vision?*

Water covered her face. She gasped, and water poured down her throat before she slammed her lips together. Her arms and legs flailed, sloshing water over the sides of the tub. She sat up, spitting water and panting for air.

The door slammed open, and Sebastian stared down at her. "What happened?" He opened the drain on the tub and grabbed a towel.

"Vision."

He frowned, handed her the towel, and turned his back. She stood and wrapped the towel around herself.

"Decent?"

"Yeah." She climbed out of the tub.

Sebastian snagged another towel, blew out the candles, and wrapped the towel and his arm around her shoulders. "Come on. Lie down on the bed. You can tell me about your vision while I clean up the water on the floor."

Willow glanced down at the puddles on the tile. "I'll get it."

He directed her to the bed. "I don't want you to slip. Sit."

"I need to call Cory. They've found her. Miles and Miranda have found her."

Sebastian grimaced, nodded, and handed Willow her phone from the nightstand. Her hands shook as she dialed.

"Hey, Willow. I was just thinking about you."

"Cory, they're coming. They know you're with one of Finn's friends from the army."

"Air Force."

"What?"

"Finn was in the Air Force. Are you sure?"

"Yes, you have to get out of there." Fear made her voice tremble.

"Okay. I'll ditch this phone and call you from a new one when we're on the road."

"Good idea."

"Are you safe where you are?"

"I think so."

"Then we'll stick to the plan. Bye."

The phone disconnected, and Willow dropped it in her lap. Sebastian stood in front of her.

"They'll make their way here."

He nodded. "Tell me your vision."

She told him about inducing the vision to locate Justin's family and how it switched to Miranda and Miles. "I think it might've been because I started thinking about family. Or it could've been to warn me. Or both." Willow raised her head. "Sebastian, Miranda sensed me. She knew it was me watching her. She said she'd see me soon and teach me some manners. How did she know? You don't think she could've read my mind in a vision, do you? Could she have seen our location?"

"Before today, I would've said no, but you said Justin's sister sensed you too. Miranda's a telepath and connected to you, so it's not far-fetched she could sense you. The question is why now, and could she do more than sense your presence?"

"We should leave, shouldn't we?" *It isn't safe. I'll have to tell Cory when she calls again.*

"Get dressed and grab your go bag. I'll grab mine and wipe our presence."

"I have to call Justin."

Sebastian stopped in the doorway.

Willow shook her head. "Don't even try to talk me out of it."

"I wasn't going to. Tell him we'll be at his cabin within the hour. And tell him to pack." Sebastian disappeared out the door. It closed softly behind him.

What if Justin refuses to leave or doesn't want to go with us?

He had to.

She dialed his number and waited. It rang twice. *What if he doesn't pick up? Should I leave a voicemail or text? Is it safe?*

"Hey."

"Justin, we have to leave. Miranda and Miles might be on their way. You need to pack. We'll pick you up in an hour." Her words tumbled over one another.

Silence stretched.

"Justin?"

"I'll be waiting."

TWENTY-TWO

Justin grabbed his go bag from under the bed. He was always ready to disappear at a moment's notice. His mother and grandmother had instilled the necessity once he was old enough to walk and talk. It wasn't until he was older and around other kids that he realized not every kid slept with a backpack filled with clothes and their most cherished possessions under their bed. The backpack had morphed into a duffel bag when he'd become an adult and set out on his own, but it still held clothes and a few prized possessions along with a handful of different identifications and currencies. He scanned the contents to ensure everything was there. His fingers paused over the smooth back of the little wooden bear statue his mother had given him for his seventh birthday. He'd had a mild obsession, for a time, after seeing one in a zoo. It had been a while since he'd looked at the carving. He tucked it back into the shawl he'd bought for his grandmother but had never been able to give her.

He tossed the bag on the counter and emptied the fridge of perishables. There was no telling how long he would be gone or if he would ever come back.

Less than ten minutes had passed when he hefted the duffel over his shoulder and shut and locked the cabin door. He walked across the yard to the path meandering through the woods and glanced over his shoulder.

The cabin nestled into the forest of towering trees had given him a small sense of peace. If he got his revenge and ended his lifelong battle, he would return. It was one of the few spots on earth he'd found that felt like he might belong.

He shifted the bag on his shoulder and walked down the trail. Pine needles edged the dirt path. His worn boots brushed against rocks and tree roots protruding from the ground. Willow's brother and sister were close if Willow's warning was to be believed. He had no reason not to believe her—unless she was as evil as the rest of her family and it had been all part of some twisted plot to get close to him. *But then why the warning?*

He could simply disappear instead of waiting for Willow and Sebastian to arrive. Stay on his own. It had kept him alive that long.

Willow was too sweet and open to deceive or betray him like that. It wasn't in her nature. Her brother, on the other hand, was more than capable of deception.

Justin grimaced and tightened his fingers on the straps of his duffel. They had told him a good story about fighting their own family. *But is that all it was, a tall tale?*

Willow had helped him with his powers. Even Sebastian had helped in his own way. *Why would either of them have done that if they intended to betray me?* It didn't make sense. It would take a real twisted individual to play with him like a cat playing with a mouse before killing it.

He would lose all faith and trust in his instincts if they betrayed him. They were still his best path to avenging his mother and grandmother. Revenge was a powerful motivator to stay right where he was and let Miles and Miranda come to him. He could set a trap and battle them on his turf.

Willow hadn't said how she knew her siblings were coming. *Did she have a vision?*

He would wait for their arrival and get some answers before he decided to stay or go.

She'd admitted her visions required a certain degree of interpretation. He didn't understand how they worked. She claimed his father was out there with an extended family, happily living his life. He could've gone on without knowing that the man who'd abandoned his pregnant mother was living a blissful life while she had been tortured and murdered.

Power vibrated beneath his skin.

Justin calmed his mind and slowed his breathing. *I control my magic. It doesn't control me.* His tension eased, and the power dissipated.

If Willow's visions were indeed of his father and he had siblings out there, he wanted to meet them. He didn't care about his father. The man had made his choice. He had wanted nothing to do with Justin or his mother. But his siblings might not know about his existence. Them, he would give a chance. If they didn't want anything to do with him, either, so be it.

A thick root bisected the path, and he stepped over it. His mother wouldn't have lied to him about his father. Justin stopped and gazed down the winding path ahead. *Not unless she was protecting me from something.*

She'd never said his father was a witch. *Could he be evil like Willow's father? If we search for my possible family, would we be adding to the danger surrounding us?*

He kicked a small pebble off the path as he walked on. Willow hoped that locating the subjects of her visions would give them more allies, but it could very well add to their list of enemies.

It was probably best to deal with one problem at a time. He would wait until he got his vengeance on Willow's father, then he could search for his possible siblings or other relatives.

Stopping before the path's last turn, he reached the small

parking lot that held his Jeep. Justin listened and searched his surroundings for any threat or presence. Only the normal sounds and sights of the forest reached him. He let loose small tendrils of his power like Willow had shown him to search for hidden dangers or other witches. He closed his eyes and tilted his head back as he connected with the trees and ground beneath his feet. A soothing peace echoed back to him. He was alone.

The duffel kicked up a small cloud of dust when he dropped it next to the wheel of his Jeep and unlocked the door. He tossed the duffel in the back then leaned against the side of the vehicle with the door open. Willow and Sebastian should arrive soon. They were probably almost as accustomed as him to leaving a place quickly.

He would listen to their plan then decide what was best for him.

The distant hum of an engine and tires traversing the parking lot's dirt road reached his ears. He paused a second to note any differences between the sounds and the previous ones that had announced Willow and Sebastian's arrival at his home. They seemed the same.

As a precaution, he started his Jeep and stood ready to jump in and leave in a hurry. He hadn't picked up on anything, but Willow could have made the call under duress.

The familiar sedan pulled in with Sebastian behind the wheel and Willow in the passenger seat. She gave him a tremulous smile while her brother had his familiar scowl locked in place.

Willow jumped out of the car as soon as it stopped. "Thank the stars! I've been so worried." She hustled across the distance and practically threw herself into his arms. "I had a vision. Miranda and Miles know where Cory and Finn are, and Miranda knew I was having a vision of them. She might track us here."

Justin hugged her. "But you're not sure?"

She pulled back and shook her head. "No, I told Cory to come here, but then I realized Miranda might have the ability to reach into my mind in a vision. She's a powerful telepath. I don't know what she's capable of."

"We've been here too long anyway." Sebastian folded his arms over his chest and leaned against the hood of the car. "It's time to move on. I've got a place set up. We've already told Cory to meet us there instead. All that remains is for you to decide to follow us or not." He shrugged. "Up to you."

Willow frowned at her brother. "Sebastian, we discussed this."

"Yeah, you and I have, but it's still his decision whether he joins us or not."

Willow turned and stared up at him. "You are coming with us, aren't you?"

"What exactly was your vision? It's quite a leap to assume they're coming here, isn't it? Besides, what if they are? We can prepare a trap for them here."

She started shaking her head before he'd even finished talking. "It's not safe. We're not ready to face them. We all need to be together and come up with a plan. And... there's more. The vision started with your father. I was looking for him before it switched to Miranda and Miles. Justin, I think your father is in San Francisco." Willow clutched his arms as she told him about her vision.

He had a location and a nephew. A place to start after they dealt with Miles and Miranda.

She sucked in a breath. "You and I should go to San Francisco to find them." She glanced over her shoulder. "Sebastian, you go meet Cory and Finn in Seattle. We'll all meet up afterward. Hopefully, we'll have reinforcements with us from Justin's family."

"Absolutely not!" Sebastian surged to a stand and glared at them.

Justin shook his head at the same time. "No."

Willow glanced between them with a frown. "Why not? We need all the help we can get."

"You're not going off on a wild-goose chase alone with him. We need to prepare for Cory and Finn's arrival and come up with a plan to thwart Miles and Miranda."

Willow turned and put her hands on her hips. "Sebastian, do I really need to remind you I'm a grown woman who can take care of herself? Or that I can make my own decisions about who I trust to travel with?"

The scowl on Sebastian's face deepened.

Justin cleared his throat. The last thing they needed was for her brother to lose his temper and throw a fit over a pointless argument. "While I agree you can take care of yourself and make your own decisions, I don't agree we should go looking for anyone. My mother wouldn't talk about him for a reason. He could be dangerous. They all could. For all we know, they could be as evil as your family."

Willow gaped at him and shook her head. "My visions showed a happy family. One filled with love. Evil cannot exist among so much love. There was never any love in my family except with Basty."

Sebastian stared off into the woods. "Love and evil can coexist. Just because someone is capable of love doesn't mean they're not equally capable of evil. You always see the good in people, Willow. But there is almost always bad too."

Willow sighed. "I'm not that naïve. I choose to look for the good, but that doesn't mean I don't know the bad exists. I wasn't planning on blindly approaching Justin's family. We would be careful and exercise extreme caution." She turned and put her hand on Justin's arm. "I'm not disparaging your mother in any way. I'm sure she had her reasons, but we don't know them. She might not have known either. We have no way of knowing what kind of man or witch he is until we find and observe him. People's auras have a darkness when they're evil—like Edward's. I didn't see that in my visions. I'm not saying it's foolproof, but it's a sign. I feel this is the right step to take. Please trust me." Her eyes pleaded with him.

We could locate them without contact. We could observe from a distance. Willow's abilities would aid us.

Sebastian reclined against the hood of the car once again and crossed his ankles. "She's right. I don't like it, but she is."

Justin nodded. "We do nothing but observe unless I say otherwise. This is my blood. I'll make the final decision."

"Agreed." Willow held out her hand to shake, a little smile quivering across her lips.

He shook her hand with a sigh and prayed he wouldn't regret looking for his family.

Willow kissed him on the cheek and skipped over to the car. She hefted a backpack and tote from the back seat.

Justin moved to help her, but Sebastian stepped in front of him. "I'm trusting you with my sister. Let any harm come to her, and there isn't a place on this planet I won't find and destroy you."

Justin thought about rolling his eyes at the threat, but he knew Sebastian meant every word. *If I had a sister, and it seems I do, would I feel the same protectiveness?* They didn't know one another, but something stirred inside him at the thought of her existence. "Message received. I'll protect her with my life. I would have anyway, with or without the threat."

Sebastian nodded. "See that you do."

Willow removed another tote from the car and put it with her other bags in the back of his Jeep. He lifted a brow and glanced at the bags.

She gave him an impish grin and shrugged. "The totes are just extra clothes. I can and will ditch them if necessary."

A smirk twitched at his lips.

She walked over and hugged her brother. "No more threats. I'll be fine. You just worry about Cory and Finn arriving and thinking up a plan to deal with Miles and Miranda if they find us. I'm sure we'll join you in a few days. I have a strong sense of where Justin's family is located. We'll check in every day, okay?"

Sebastian kissed her on the forehead and escorted her around the back of the Jeep to the passenger door. "Don't forget the code words."

"I won't. You don't forget to check in either."

He nodded and stared across the interior of the Jeep at Justin. "Willow knows the address in Seattle. Commit it to memory. Don't write it down or record it anywhere."

Justin raised his eyebrows. *A sign of trust?* Then again, Sebastian was already trusting him with the only person he seemed to care about. *What is an address compared to that?* "Understood. Watch your back."

"Same. You know how to travel undetected and not leave a trail?"

"I've been doing it all my life."

Sebastian stared at Willow for a moment before he shut her door and walked to his car and got in. By the time Justin climbed into his Jeep and put on his seat belt, Sebastian had reversed and disappeared down the dirt road. A cloud of dust floated in his wake.

Justin put his hand on the gearshift, and Willow reached over and entwined their fingers.

"This is the right decision. I feel it."

He gave her a smile and followed her brother from the parking lot. By the time he reached the main road, there was no sign of Sebastian. He hoped Willow was right. But luck and hope had never been on his side before. He doubted anything had changed.

CHAPTER

TWENTY-THREE

The chilly wind lashed at Justin's hair and face as he stood on the hotel balcony. His fingers clenched the metal railing. He'd seen his father with his own eyes. He was no longer some abstract apparition from Willow's vision. Justin could no longer deny his existence.

He had no clue how he felt about it. Other than that he was angry.

He and Willow had only taken a day to locate him. The man, Arthur, had been laughing and playing frisbee in a park with his grandchild. Justin had driven away without a word while Willow pleaded with him to stop so they wouldn't lose track of him.

He hadn't stopped. He couldn't.

The sperm donor had wanted nothing to do with him or his mother. *What's different about this family that made him want them? And why do I give a damn about a man I've never known?*

The whole situation was out of control. All he wanted was revenge against his mother's murderer. He hadn't wanted to know anything about his father. He hadn't wanted to get involved with a coven or get mixed up with Willow.

Justin pushed off the balcony and strode into the hotel room. He slammed the sliding door behind him and stalked into his bedroom. They'd gotten a two-bedroom suite. She'd shot him a look that he had no idea how to interpret when he'd requested it at the front desk. *Did she expect a separate room?* Hell if he knew what she wanted. She'd disappeared into her room and had been abnormally quiet all morning while they'd searched the area.

Until they'd located Arthur and his family. Then she'd instructed him to go back to the hotel while she picked up some supplies. He'd started to argue with her, but after his anger had triggered his power to topple a tree, he'd gone. She shouldn't have trouble making a quick stop at a store. Her family wasn't looking for her there. She would be back any minute.

He stared at his duffel on the chair in the corner. The whole situation was too intense. He needed to clear his head.

Justin grabbed his duffel and headed for the door. She had his number. If she ran into any trouble, she could call him. She would be fine, though. She could get herself back to Sebastian without help from him.

But when he opened the hotel door, Willow stood at the threshold. She glanced at his bag then raised her gaze back to his face. She walked past him and placed the bags on the table. He turned and watched her unpack the items and line them up in a neat row and a small pile.

"Don't stay on my account. If you want to leave, then leave."

He sighed. *What am I doing?* He didn't know what the hell he wanted. "I feel like I'm jumping out of my skin here. I'm afraid I'm so keyed up I'll start an earthquake or something."

She folded her arms under her breasts and faced him. "There's more than one way to release energy. Give your thoughts and emotions another direction to focus. You don't have to run."

He dropped his duffel and held out his arms. "What do you suggest? Because I'm all ears."

"Why did you request a two-bedroom when we checked in?"

He shook his head. "I knew it. You were pissed. Why didn't you just say you wanted your own room?" He slapped his hands on his hips. "I don't think arguing is an effective way to calm my emotions or powers."

"I don't want to fight, and I didn't want my own room."

"Then spell it out for me because I don't have a clue where your mind is at."

Willow unbuttoned the top button on her blouse.

His gaze locked on the opening gap as she unbuttoned the next. "What are you doing?"

"Giving your... passions another focus."

He rubbed his hand over his suddenly slack jaw. *Is she offering what I think she is?*

Her fingers halted on the last button as her shirt fell open to reveal a light-pink bra cupping the tempting swells of her breasts. "Unless you're not interested? Is that why you got the two-bedroom instead of one?"

"You know damn well I'm interested. I was trying not to make assumptions and be a gentleman. I didn't... I don't want to rush you."

She removed her blouse, and his mouth watered.

"You're not rushing me. I want this. I want you."

He should slow things down. She was too innocent and sheltered. He didn't want to take advantage of her.

She sauntered toward him. "You're coming up with a list of reasons not to, aren't you? Unless one of them is because you're not attracted to me..."

He glanced down at his obvious erection. "Pretty sure the evidence of my attraction is clear."

Her cheeks pinkened, and she smiled. "In that case, stop thinking and feel." Her arms encircled his neck.

The softness of her lush lips pressed against his as her tongue tentatively entangled with his own. Her body plastered along his from chest to thighs. He rested his hands at the small of her back.

The fact that she was a virgin and inexperienced blared in the forefront of his mind. The gentlemanly thing to do would be to tell her to wait for someone she loved and who loved her in return. He cared for her, but he wasn't capable of loving someone.

The warmth of her skin seeped through his clothes. His thumbs brushed over the indent in the small of her back.

She was a grown woman. *If she wants this, who am I to grow a conscience?* He'd been very clear about his lack of intentions from the start. She knew he wouldn't stick around for long.

"Stop thinking so hard." She nuzzled his neck and whispered in his ear, "You're the one acting like a virgin, standing so stiff and barely touching me." She latched onto his earlobe and bit softly.

The sensation went straight to his groin.

He cupped her cheeks in his palms and stared into her sparkling eyes. "So be it." He crushed his lips against hers and delved into her mouth with his tongue.

Willow melted against him. He scooped her up and stalked to the bedroom.

She bit her lip and grinned. "This is more like it."

He chuckled and shook his head slightly as he lowered her to the bed. Her blouse fell to her sides, baring her to his gaze. Her small breasts plumped over the edge of the pink bra. *She's a sexy little nymph.*

Justin tugged his shirt over his head.

Willow's gaze scanned his chest as a little smile pursed her lips. She unbuttoned her pants and wiggled them off. Her panties matched her bra and were a tiny scrap of nothing that he could probably rip with his bare hands.

"Why'd you stop? Remove those jeans, cowboy."

He tilted his head. "Cowboy? I've never been on a horse in my life."

She shrugged as a little giggle escaped her. "Seemed to fit with you standing there in your jeans with your naked chest and muscular abs making my mouth water." She tossed her pants and shirt on the end of the bed and leaned back on her elbows. "On with the show."

He couldn't stop the grin that spread over his mouth as she comically wiggled her eyebrows and winked. Her gaze dropped as soon as he unbuttoned his jeans. The smile slowly faded from her face as he got a condom, tossed it on the bed, and slid both his jeans and briefs off together.

Is she nervous? He kicked them to the side.

She licked her lips. A slight flush spread over her chest, turning the white pillows of her breasts a light pink to match her bra and panties. Her chest rose and fell with quickened breaths.

"You can change your mind at any time, Willow."

She removed her bra and panties in response.

He sucked in a hard breath. *She's perfect.*

Justin covered her body with his. She sighed and smoothed her palms up his arms and over his shoulders. Kissing her deeply, he propped himself up with one arm so he could explore her body with his free hand. He loved how she responded to his touch. She angled closer to his hand wherever it roamed and let loose with little sighs or moans teaching him what she liked.

He was determined to make it good for her no matter how hard it was for his body to wait. A thin layer of perspiration already coated his skin from the strain. He watched her body twitch and squirm as pleasure doused her and took over.

Willow's eyes slid closed, and her neck arched. Soft gasps escaped her open mouth. Her eyes inched open, and she smiled. She watched avidly as he donned the condom and slowly joined their bodies. Heat raced down his spine. Her eyes widened, then her lids slid seductively low as she clasped him to her.

Every movement brought ecstasy. His thoughts scattered, and a low groan built in his throat. Her body clenched around him, finding its release. The orgasm crashed into him like a semi without brakes. He caught himself as he collapsed onto her chest, his body spent. His arms quivered slightly.

His gaze collided with hers as he fought to catch his breath. She stared at him with wonderment stamped across her flushed face.

What have I done?

TWENTY-FOUR

Justin drove into the next San Francisco neighborhood with one hand on the steering wheel and the other propped in the open window of the Jeep. His body leaned against the driver's door.

He couldn't get farther from Willow unless he drove from outside the vehicle. He'd grown increasingly distant over the past two days as they'd searched one neighborhood after another surrounding the park where they'd seen his father. So far, she hadn't been able to identify the house where she'd seen his father in her vision.

At least they knew the general location—unless he'd been visiting from somewhere else. She didn't want to mention the possibility since Justin was already beating himself up over leaving instead of confronting his father. She didn't blame him for his reaction to seeing his father for the first time.

Willow turned her gaze to the houses towering over the street. Most had little or no lawn to speak of out front. Occasionally, she glimpsed one with a decent-sized lot, but the houses themselves or shrubbery often blocked views of the backyard if there was one.

She would like to think his distance had to do with finding or not finding his father, but since he'd avoided any intimacy between them since they had sex, she had to assume it was her. *Is he the one-and-done sort of man?* She knew he wasn't interested in a long-term relationship, but she had at least thought they would continue to have sex while they were in San Francisco.

Her insecurities had gotten the best of her when she'd woken that first night to find him gone. When he finally returned, he'd slept on the couch rather than his bed, which she'd still been occupying. She'd moved back to her bedroom the following night, after his continued distance.

Books and movies had given her enough knowledge to know he'd found pleasure with her. *So, what's the problem? Is he worried I'll get too attached? Does he just not want a repeat performance?*

"Anything look familiar?"

She started at his low grumble of a voice. Considering he hadn't spoken more than a few words to her all day, she might've questioned whether he'd lost the power of speech.

"No, sorry. They're all melting together a bit, to be honest."

He grunted and turned at the stop sign.

She sighed audibly. She'd lost count of the number of streets they had driven up and down. With their luck, one of the residents would report them to the police for suspicious activity.

"Look, if this is the way you intend to act the rest of the time we're here, it's going to become intolerable. What exactly is your problem?" She folded her arms over her waist and glared at him, waiting for a response.

He gave her a brief side glance before he returned his gaze to the road.

Is he really just going to ignore me? She gritted her teeth and stared out the window.

"It never should have happened. I don't want to hurt you."

Willow rolled her eyes. "Pretty damn arrogant of you to assume I'm the one who will end up hurt. Men! Why does anyone have to get hurt? I don't have any expectations except maybe civility. Do you? Do you really believe that all women are just waiting for some man to pay them a little attention and, if they do, then the women start to weave happily-ever-after fantasies around them? I gave up believing in fairy tales a long time ago. Unless you're talking about the original stories that are dark and not the least bit happily ever after. Those I've had plenty of firsthand experience with."

Justin snorted. "You look so sweet and innocent. I forget there's a little spitfire inside the package." He rubbed the back of his neck. "I'm sorry, okay? I admit I've been spinning these thoughts inside my head. You're right. It was rather presumptuous of me."

Her lips quirked. "Did you really think I would go off and buy his-and-her T-shirts or something? Or drag you to go ring shopping? I told you I just want to experience life while I can. Is it so wrong to enjoy the time we have?"

"I guess not." Justin's gaze ran over her. "What do you say we take a break from the search and head back to the hotel?"

"I should punish you for being so hardheaded the past couple of days, but that would be punishing myself too." She winked at him. "I'm game to play hooky."

He grinned and glanced in the rearview mirror before flipping the turn signal to head back to the hotel.

Willow sighed softly and leaned back against the seat. With the issue resolved, maybe they could both relax and have a chance to enjoy each other while it lasted. She knew their journey would be short-lived. At any moment, her family could find her and drag her back to her previous hell. But she was determined to enjoy her freedom and experience every bit of life she could squeeze out during whatever time she had.

A tension seeped into her shoulders, and an awareness sparked inside her. "Stop the Jeep!"

Justin slammed on the brakes.

Willow slapped her hand on the dash as the seat belt caught and stopped her forward momentum. She searched both sides of the street.

"What is it?"

A brown three-story house with wide stairs and a front porch stood just behind them. She sucked in a breath. "That's it. That's the house."

"How can you be sure?"

She glanced at Justin and back to the house. "It's hard to explain. I just know. But the color does match my vision, now that I see it. Before, I wasn't quite sure what the house looked like because I was so focused on your father and the location. But I see it clearly now." Willow recounted the vision in her head, cataloging details. It had to be the house. Every signal in her body told her it was.

"So, what's the plan? Do we just knock on the door and say, 'Hi, you don't know me, but my friend here is a witch and has visions. And in one of these visions, she happened to see my sperm donor lived here. We're looking for him because there are these bad guys chasing us and we were wondering if he could help since, apparently, he might be a witch too'? Do you think they'll call the police before or after they slam the door in our faces?"

"I guess we should've discussed this beforehand. I don't think that approach is a sound one." Willow turned to Justin with a smile. "But since he is a witch, it might not sound so far-fetched."

He simply lifted an eyebrow and stared at her.

A flash of movement preceded a hard knock on the hood of the Jeep. Willow jumped as she swung her head around. Long mahogany-brown hair and round brown eyes—it was the woman from her visions. She had a hard look about her as she glared at them.

"Who are you, and what do you want?" The woman's eyes narrowed as her gaze swept over them.

Justin put his hand over Willow's, which was clutching the side of her seat. "I'll handle this. Hopefully, she hasn't already called the police about us lurking. I don't relish trying to explain it to the authorities." He lowered his window.

"Wait, Justin." *He doesn't know who she is.*

He glanced at her and frowned.

She leaned close and whispered, "She was in my visions."

His head snapped back to the woman, who tilted her head just like Justin had so many times before. They stared at one another through the windshield.

Willow swallowed hard and rubbed her clammy hands on her pants. She was Justin's sister. Willow knew it from the visions, but after seeing them together, there wasn't a doubt in her mind. They shared a strong resemblance.

She didn't know the woman's name, but she recalled the witch's power. She'd sensed Willow even in the vision, and she'd sent birds flying after her. The green aura surrounding her confirmed she was a witch, and a powerful one by the thick, bright aura. *Does she sense who and what we were? Can she identify other witches? Does she know about Justin?*

Willow snuck a peek at Justin. He and his sister were still locked in some sort of staring battle. *What are they thinking?*

That wasn't getting them anywhere. She sighed and got out of the car.

Justin reached for her. "Willow, get back in the car. What are you doing?"

She gave him a reassuring smile and turned her smile toward his sister. "Hello. We seem to have gotten off on the wrong foot. My name is Willow. What's yours?"

His sister barely spared her a glance before returning her gaze to Justin.

Is it possible she doesn't know we're witches? Not everyone knew how to recognize other witches. *Does she think we're scouting the area to rob it or something? Why else would she confront us if she doesn't know what we were?*

Justin got out of the Jeep and frowned at Willow. "Get back in the car."

Willow folded her arms. "No." She really was sick of everyone telling her what to do. If she left it up to him, they would probably still be sitting in the Jeep, having a staring contest with each other.

"Willow..."

His sister glanced between the two of them. "You haven't answered my question."

Something growled behind Willow. She whirled and spotted a large dog less than ten feet away. Another appeared across the street.

Yup, her power is definitely animals.

Justin ran behind the vehicle and stood in front of her. "Get back into the Jeep. Slowly."

Willow turned with her back against his and faced his sister. "This really isn't necessary. We only want to talk. Please call them off before someone gets hurt."

"Is that a threat?"

"No."

"Yes," Justin said at the same time.

The woman's lips moved, and two more dogs appeared, running down the road toward them.

Where are they coming from? Is the woman casting spells to bring all the dogs in the city here?

"Will you both stand down before this escalates further?" Willow planted her hands on her hips. *Is no one capable of being reasonable anymore?*

Birds landed in the trees lining the street and on the house roofs. Justin tensed against her back.

Please don't let him cause an earthquake. They would really make a terrible impression on his newfound family then.

Willow sighed. "You can call every animal in the city if it makes you feel better, but we really just want to talk." She reached back, took Justin's hand, and gave it what she hoped was a reassuring squeeze. "Isn't that right, Justin?"

"That depends on whether any of her circus act decide to attack."

Willow closed her eyes briefly. She needed to alleviate the tension. "Justin's your brother. We're here to talk to your father."

TWENTY-FIVE

Justin's fingers tightened on Willow's almost painfully. The ground rumbled beneath them. The dogs whined. Some ran. The birds took flight. Car alarms blared up and down the street and in the distance. His sister's eyes widened, and she flung her arms wide, staring at the ground.

Willow whirled and wrapped her arms around Justin from behind. "It's okay. Breathe. Let it dissipate."

The orange door of the brown house flung open, and the man from her visions came racing down the steps. Arthur, his father.

Oh no! Justin isn't prepared for this. Please, don't let him see his father yet! She jumped in front of Justin and grabbed his face to make him focus on her. *Too late.* His gaze was riveted on his father. "Justin..."

"I'm fine." He took hold of her hands and moved her behind him. He backed her up until she was wedged between him and the car.

She placed her hands on his wide back and peered around him to his sister, who stood on the sidewalk watching Justin like he was a specimen beneath a microscope.

Arthur stopped next to her, huffing. "Rena, are you all right?"

So, that's her name.

Rena nodded without taking her eyes off Justin.

Arthur glanced at Justin and frowned. "There might be after-shocks." He took his daughter's hand. "We should get inside." He raised his chin toward Justin. "I suggest you two do the same."

"It was him." Rena flung her hand at Justin. "It wasn't an earthquake. He did it. He's a witch. And she claims he's my brother. They came here for you."

Arthur's mouth opened and closed. He took two steps toward Justin. "Son?"

Justin had turned to stone in front of Willow. She pushed lightly on his back, but he didn't move or respond.

Willow angled her head farther out. "Hi there. I'm Willow, and this is Justin."

A car honked and drove around them.

She looked at their surroundings. Justin's Jeep was still parked in the middle of the street. A couple of neighbors stood outside looking in their direction. "Perhaps we could discuss this inside? Or at least off the street? We're attracting attention."

"Of course." Arthur waved a hand toward his house.

"Dad! We don't know anything about these people. You're not inviting them into your house. Wait... Do you know them?" Rena stared up at her father.

Willow waited to hear Arthur's response. *Did he know about Justin?* His earlier reaction didn't exactly confirm or deny anything.

"No, but if he claims to be my son, then I think it's best to get to know him, don't you? The young lady is correct. We are attracting unwanted attention. I see no reason we can't be civilized and go inside to straighten this out."

"He caused an earthquake! I'd say that's reason enough not to invite him into your house."

"You had a pack of dogs growling at us, ready to attack, and flocks of birds preparing to pluck our eyes out or some-thing. At the risk of sounding immature... you started it." Willow waved a hand in the air. "Besides, it was just a brief rumble. Hardly qualifies as an earthquake. No need to be dramatic."

Justin finally moved by glancing over his shoulder and giving her an incredulous look.

She shrugged and patted his back. "I'll move your Jeep off the street." She darted around him and the Jeep, tossing a jaunty wave in his father's and sister's direction.

Arthur stared at her with a slight smile while Rena glared at her like she was contemplating calling back the dogs.

Willow warily glanced around as she climbed into the Jeep. They were probably lurking in the bushes or something, waiting for a signal to attack. She would never look at animals the same way again.

<hr>

Justin watched Willow get in his Jeep out of the corner of his eye while he kept his attention on the man and woman in front of him. No way did he think of them as family. At best, they were strangers. At worst, they were dangerous enemies.

Arthur stepped forward and held out his hand. "It seems you already know, but I'm Arthur Diaz. And you're Justin…"

He stared at the offered hand like it was a snake poised to strike. *The sperm donor wants to shake hands like we're acquaintances meeting on the street?*

Arthur cleared his throat and dropped his arm.

Rena stalked between them and tilted her head back to glare at Justin. Her lesser height diminished the threatening effect she was clearly going for. He had almost a foot on her.

Willow came to them at a run after finding a parking spot down the street. "Well now, didn't you mention taking this inside—off the street—away from prying eyes?" She smiled sunnily at the three of them, grabbed his hand, and tugged him onto the sidewalk.

"Right you are, Willow, wasn't it?" Arthur returned her smile and waved a hand for them to precede him.

Like hell. Justin wouldn't allow either of them at his back. He kept his feet planted where they were.

Willow nodded and tugged at his hand, but he shook his head at her.

"We'll follow you."

Rena fisted her hands and propped them on her hips. "If you think for one minute that we'll turn our backs to you—"

"Now, Rena..." Arthur put a hand on her shoulder.

"Right back at you, little she-devil."

Rena gasped and took a step toward him.

Willow threw up a placating hand. "Maybe you two could save this sibling rivalry for inside?"

"He's not my brother. I don't know what the two of you are up to, but you're failing at whatever con you're running here. I've already alerted my *real* brothers, and they're on their way."

"That might be for the best, little bit, but not for the reason you think." Arthur sighed heavily. "I suspect Justin is very much your brother. I'd like to think there's a resemblance between us."

"Just because the bloke has dark hair and tan skin doesn't make him a relation. Plenty of people can say they share a resemblance. It doesn't make them blood."

"The resemblance goes beyond skin or hair color, don't you think?" Willow gestured between Arthur and Justin. "Actually, Justin's hair is darker than Arthur's."

Arthur smiled slightly. "He has Maria's hair and her nose, doesn't he?"

Every muscle in Justin's body clenched at hearing his mother's name on the sperm donor's lips. One question answered. He'd known. His mother hadn't lied about that.

Willow's hand stroked down his back.

"Don't worry. I don't want a damn thing from you. I only came here for Willow's sake. You can go back to pretending I don't exist after she has her say."

Willow and Arthur both sucked in a breath.

Rena stared at her father with wide eyes. "Dad?"

"I never pretended you didn't exist. I hoped Maria wouldn't go through with her threats. I prayed on it every day for months until I knew that, if you had survived, you would've been born. Then my prayers turned to your health and hoping you'd come looking for me one day. It's why I never moved away from San Francisco. I wanted to make it as easy as possible for Maria and you to find me if you ever wanted to."

"Easy for you to blame my mother now that she's not around to defend herself. You expect me to believe she threatened to abort me? Or what, give me up for adoption? You expect me to believe your words over my own mother's? She was there. You weren't."

"Maria's gone?" Arthur appeared genuinely shocked and distressed.

He could be a talented actor. Or maybe he is upset to hear she died. That doesn't mean he's telling the truth about anything else. Justin folded his arms over his chest and gave a curt nod. "A long time ago."

"I... I swear to you I didn't know. I'm not trying to tarnish your mother's memory. I'm only speaking my truth. My wife, Annie, can confirm I told her the same many years ago, before we married and started a family. She knew I longed and prayed for you. I knew Maria was frightened, and I'd hoped the feeling would pass and she would come back, but after a couple of years..." He held out his hands and dropped them. "I met my Annie."

Rena put her hand on her father's arm. "Dad, you have no proof this is him. You're giving away too much information. They could be con artists."

Willow raised her chin. "A simple DNA test will confirm Justin is his son. It's not like we could play the ruse for long in this day and age. But you're both witches of the earth, and so is Justin. He looks just like a younger version of Arthur. I think those two facts are enough to give him the benefit of the doubt and stop treating him like a criminal."

"Please forgive any offense. My daughter is very protective. She knows how long I've waited for this day. Over the years, we've had a few attempts from less-than-trustworthy individuals to convince me they were my long-lost son. In the beginning, I hired private detectives and put up flyers. It brought nothing but scam artists." He turned his gaze to Justin. "There is no doubt in my mind Justin is my son, but for my daughter's sake, we should probably do a DNA test."

"We've got a test inside. We started keeping them on hand when the con artists showed up. Mom replaces them like clockwork every six months, so they're not expired. All you need to do is swab your cheek." Rena lifted her eyebrows. "Any issues with providing some spit?"

A brief image of spitting at her feet crossed his mind, but he was willing to be civil if she was. *The sooner we get this over with, the sooner Willow and I can get the hell out of here.* "Lead the way."

She hesitated a second, no doubt thinking of their previous battle of who would follow who, but she stalked down the sidewalk, gritting her teeth so hard she probably created grooves.

Arthur smiled hesitantly before turning and following his daughter.

Willow put her hand on Justin's arm and smiled up at him. "I know this is hard for you. And if it's too much, we can leave right now. But I really think you should hear him out. He seems genuine, and I don't get any sense of falsehood from him or her. I'm not an expert like my sister, but I can usually tell if someone is trying to deceive me. It was a necessary skill to hone growing up in my household."

Sometimes, he forgot her family situation was worse than his. *Unless Arthur and his family are hiding evil secrets too.*

CHAPTER
TWENTY-SIX

Dozens of family photos covered the white walls of the living room. It was like catching glimpses of their lives all around him. It painted a picture of a tight, happy family. But pictures could hide lies behind the smiling faces. They only captured a moment in time. Anyone could post pictures of a happy family. It didn't always tell the story.

Justin stood just inside the front door. Part of him wanted to walk away, but a small part of him wanted to hear what Arthur had to say. He didn't feel a connection to them. They weren't his family.

Rena had produced a DNA test as soon as they'd walked in the door. He'd swabbed his cheek and followed the directions. She'd taken the test and disappeared down the hall. Arthur had told them to make themselves at home and had gone into the kitchen.

Willow kept glancing at Justin as if worried he would bolt or lose control of his magic and destroy the house. His mother used to watch him similarly.

She smiled and slipped her hand into his. "You okay? We can still leave at any time."

"What about your plan?"

She shrugged. "Plans can change. We don't know if they could help, let alone if they'd be willing. Your peace of mind is more important."

He studied her features. She seemed sincere. She would walk away with him if he asked.

"I'm fine. I want to hear what he has to say."

Willow could make her pitch about forming a coven. Then they could leave.

Arthur and Rena entered the room carrying drinks and a tray of cookies.

"Annie is a much better hostess than I am, but I thought we could all use refreshments." Arthur put the tray on the table and handed Willow and Justin each a glass of iced tea.

He took the glass, but he had no intention of consuming anything they offered. He nudged Willow's arm and gave a quick shake of his head when she glanced at him. She looked at the glass in her hand and frowned but nodded.

"Please, have a seat." Arthur and Rena sat in chairs on one side of the table.

Willow tugged him onto the couch opposite them. He sat on the edge and rested his hands on his knees. He wanted to tell them to get it over with and tell him what he wanted to know. *Why do people need to sit through useless pleasantries to get to the point?*

Rena took a sip of her iced tea and placed it on a table coaster. "It takes a few weeks to get the results."

Arthur patted her knee. "Rena, I don't need the results."

"I do." Justin and Rena both spoke at the same time.

Arthur grinned. "See, like siblings already."

Rena rolled her eyes.

Justin cast his gaze around the room. He knew Arthur was his sperm donor, but he also wanted the DNA test as proof against Rena and the rest of her family's doubt.

A candle flickered inside some sort of small lamp hanging in front of a portrait. It looked religious, like Justin had seen in the church his grandmother had visited. *Some sort of shrine?*

"Saint Anthony. The patron saint of lost things. Annie put that together for me when I broke my leg and couldn't visit the church for a while. We've kept it up ever since. And now he's finally brought you back to me."

Justin's gaze shot to Arthur's. *Does he really expect me to believe that little shrine is for me?*

"I've prayed every day for your safe return." Tears filled Arthur's eyes.

Justin shot to his feet. He felt like he was poised at the edge of a cliff. His gaze darted around the room. *This isn't real.* Arthur had to be lying. There was some other explanation for that shrine. His mother hadn't lied.

The front door opened, and an older version of Rena hustled in. "Arthur, I got your message. Now, what was so urgent I had to leave work early?" She looked up and stopped in her tracks. "Oh, hello. I'm sorry. I didn't realize we had company." She smiled at him and sent a puzzled glance at Arthur. Her gaze darted back to Justin's, and she gasped. "Arthur? Is this...?"

"My son. Yes, Annie, he is."

Rena jumped to a stand. "We don't know that yet. We haven't even mailed the test out. Mom, talk some sense into him."

"Sweetheart, it's plain as day. Look at them. Besides, the heart knows, and if your father says this is his son, then he is." She stepped toward Justin and opened her arms.

Justin froze as she wrapped her arms around him in a tight hug. "Welcome home." She tilted her head back with a smile. "What's your name?"

He couldn't speak. *What is happening?*

Willow appeared beside him. "His name is Justin, and I'm Willow. This is all a lot for him to take in."

"Well, of course it is." Annie patted his arms. "Don't worry, dear. We can be a lot to handle at first, but we're family." She smiled at

Willow then turned to Arthur and Rena. "Have you called your brothers? They'll want to meet their new brother and his lady."

Rena nodded. "They'll be here any minute. Hopefully, they'll have more sense and can talk some into you two."

Annie waved her hand. "Don't mind your sister. She's the skeptic of the bunch. She wouldn't trust an angel if one showed up at the door."

"No, I wouldn't, and neither should you. Why would you trust some stranger dressed up in wings?"

"Who said an angel has to have wings?" Annie peered at the tray of cookies on the table. "I'll just take this into the kitchen and throw something more appetizing together. Everyone must be hungry." She kissed Arthur on the cheek then on the lips. "Our prayers have been answered."

Justin stared after her as she disappeared into the kitchen.

Are these people for real?

"Um, should I go see if she needs any help?" Willow pointed a finger toward the kitchen and glanced between Arthur and Rena.

Rena sighed heavily. "No, I will." She cast a glare toward Justin before she turned away.

He looked over his shoulder at the front door. *Only ten feet or so away. I could be gone in seconds. We could be.* He wouldn't leave Willow behind.

She threaded her fingers through his. "Arthur, perhaps you could tell us more about Maria. How did the two of you meet?"

Arthur smiled slightly. "On Fisherman's Wharf. She was such a beauty. She took my breath away. The passion of youth." He chuckled and gazed at the table like he saw an image from long ago.

Justin sat when Willow did.

"We weren't together long. I knew she was a witch right away, but she didn't mention it. And when she didn't bring it up, I began to suspect she didn't know I was one. I even thought maybe she didn't know she had power. She said she had no family, so I thought it was possible she didn't know anything about magic."

"She said she had no family?" Justin leaned forward. *Why would she say she was alone? She had her mother. And she knew she was a witch. Didn't she?*

Arthur frowned and nodded. "Yes, why? Was that not the truth?"

"She had my grandmother."

"Perhaps she didn't trust me enough to tell me. She didn't share much about her past."

That made sense. His mother and grandmother had taught him to keep their family secrets in the family. They trusted no one. He'd always thought it was because of him, but maybe it had started long before he was born.

"We were inseparable for about three blissful months. Until I made a mistake."

"What mistake?"

He smiled sadly. "I discovered she was pregnant with you."

"So, you admit you didn't want me?" He had tried to convince Justin it was his mother who hadn't wanted him, but she had told the truth. Arthur hadn't wanted him.

"No! It was the opposite. I was thrilled. You must understand. When I sensed the pregnancy—sensed you—I was overcome with emotion. I kissed her. I kissed her stomach. I cried." Arthur shook his head. "It took me a few moments to realize she wasn't celebrating with me. She looked at me with horror. She hadn't known she was pregnant. She did not know."

"That doesn't make any sense." *How could he possibly have known she was pregnant if she didn't?*

Willow put her hand on my leg. "He's a witch, Justin. He said he sensed you. He sensed his son."

"Exactly. At first, I didn't understand. I only felt this sense of wonderment and knowing. It was as if you said hello to me and let me know you were there. When I explained, Maria knew I was a witch, and she panicked. She said she couldn't have a witch baby. She left, and I thought she only needed some time to calm down. But I never saw her again. She disappeared. I searched everywhere, endlessly." Arthur scooted to the end of the cushion. "I always wanted you, Justin. From that first instant of awareness, you were loved."

Justin looked away from the intensity in Arthur's eyes. *Who do I believe? The woman who raised me or the man I know nothing about?*

CHAPTER
TWENTY-SEVEN

Willow smiled as she watched Justin surrounded by his newfound family. His two brothers, Frank and Noah, flanked him. They didn't have his height or muscular width, but their features marked them as brothers. They had accepted him easily, just like Arthur and Annie. It reminded her of the families she saw on television.

Rena sat in a chair alternately glaring and frowning at the lot of them. One of her adorable nephews sat on her lap, telling her what had happened at school that day. It was the same nephew who had taken the introduction to his new uncle in stride and asked Justin what sports he could play.

Justin still eyed the door from time to time, but she'd also caught a soft chuckle from him too. He was overwhelmed but handling it.

Willow spotted Rena out of the corner of her eye as she stood with a frown twisting her lips. *She won't interrupt the camaraderie with her suspicions again, will she?*

Instead of approaching the group, Rena circumvented them and headed straight for Willow.

Oh no, looks like I'm her intended target. I suppose that's better than her antagonizing Justin.

Willow pasted a smile on her face as Rena stopped beside her. The woman was several inches shorter than her and barely topped her shoulder.

"You're a psychic witch, right? You said you located Dad through your visions."

Willow had to admire her. She got straight to the point. She didn't bother hiding behind pleasantries or subtle questioning.

"Yes. As I explained to everyone over dinner, when I first had the vision of Arthur, I thought it might be of a future Justin because they looked so similar. But then, as the vision progressed, I realized I must be seeing Justin's father."

They'd been saddened but not surprised that Justin had never tried to locate his father before. *Why would he when he believed his mother that his father didn't want him?*

He had to see that for whatever her reasons, his mother had lied.

"This vision you had, describe it."

Willow turned and faced Rena fully. *What does she want to know?* "I had two, actually. The first was at a picnic in a park. The one a couple of blocks over, if I'm not mistaken. The other was on the back deck of this house. It was what led us here."

"I knew it. It was you I felt spying on us that day!"

"Yes, you sent a flock of birds flying at me. I was surprised you sensed me. Most don't. I only know of one other witch who's ever sensed me in a vision, and she's a telepath. How did you sense me? You're an earth witch. Your powers are centered around animals."

"Instinct, I guess. It's never happened before. Then again, I don't know any psychic witches capable of spying on people through visions either. You do that a lot—creepily watch people while they're unaware?"

Willow stiffened. She wasn't a stalker or anything. She hadn't intentionally sought out Arthur or his family. At least not the first time. Her shoulders slumped. Rena wasn't entirely wrong either.

Willow's family had often used her to spy on others for nefarious reasons over the years. "My visions rarely come when I want them to or show me who I expect them to. They're much too sporadic and uncontrollable to use as a means of spying on someone. Technology would be a much easier and more reliable method. I didn't mean any harm when I saw your father. I was only trying to locate him, not uncover secrets."

Rena grimaced and folded her arms under her breasts. "How does it work, then? You can't just cast a spell and have a vision of who you're looking for?"

"No, and believe me, I've tried. Sometimes, I get lucky, but more often than not, it's a pretty useless power. It's not like mind control or animal control like you have."

Rena snorted. "It doesn't always work the way I want either. Like when the animals all scattered when Justin made the ground rumble."

"Probably because you were surprised and lost focus."

"Yeah, you could say I was definitely surprised. He ever cause a real earthquake? Like falling-down buildings and all?"

Willow started to answer truthfully but paused. *Am I sharing too much?* They didn't truly know how far they could trust his family. She didn't think they meant them any harm. *But how sure am I?* She winced slightly. She'd already outed herself as basically useless when it came to power. "Justin is immensely powerful. He constantly amazes me with what he can do." She saw no reason to share that he had, indeed, caused buildings to fall. Rena also didn't need to know that he sometimes lost control of his powers, though he was getting much better.

"Dad's power is the same as mine. My brothers took after Mom and have no magic. You'd think Justin would be like us rather than manipulate the ground if he's Dad's son."

Willow almost rolled her eyes. Annie and her sons had already joked about not being witches, so Rena wasn't sharing anything new. She was pointing out, once again, why she didn't believe Justin was her brother.

"Power doesn't work that way. I have a twin brother, and though we both derive our magic from the water, he can manipulate it, where I get visions. You clearly have a lot of doubts, and you're entitled to them. I guess you'll have to wait for the test results to come back to convince you. Or will you find some other reason not to believe it then too? Maybe you should ask yourself why you refuse to accept Justin is your brother. The rest of your family knows he is. Why is it only you who continues to question it?"

She felt Justin's presence before he placed his hand on her lower back.

"Everything okay?"

She smiled up at him and leaned into his side. "Just peachy. How about you?" He didn't need to know his doubting Thomas of a sister was at it again. *Or did he hear part of the conversation?*

He glanced briefly at Rena. "Fine. I think we should head out soon. I told Arthur we'd like to speak to him privately. He suggested the backyard."

"Like hell. You're not speaking to him alone," Rena snarled.

"I figured you'd say something along those lines, which is why I mentioned it in front of you. You're the only other witch here. I don't think the kids or anyone else needs to be a party to the conversation. What you decide to divulge after the fact is up to you."

"Oh, makes sense, then." She looked around the room. "Here comes Dad." She looked at her nephew playing with one of his cousins on the floor by the fireplace. "It's something dangerous, isn't it?"

"Depends. Let's wait until we're outside." Justin took Willow's hand as they followed Arthur and Rena through the kitchen and out the back door.

The deck looked just like it had in her vision. It spanned the length of the house. They walked down the steps to the yard and followed a brick path through a vegetable and flower garden to a shed at the back of the property.

Arthur pointed to the fence behind him. "The house on the other side of this fence is empty, so I know we'll be safe from any eavesdroppers here. What did you wish to discuss? You said earlier that you came here for Willow's sake. Is that what you want to talk about?"

Justin squeezed Willow's hand. "Yes, she has a plan that needs witches to work. Maybe it's better if she explains."

Willow took a deep breath. *How am I supposed to explain everything?* It would take days to cover it all. She didn't need to tell them everything yet. They hadn't agreed to help. *Could they even help?* Rena possessed strong magic. Her abilities would be a nice addition to their coven, but it was highly doubtful she would agree. *Arthur would probably agree to help his son, but how powerful is he?*

"Without going into too many details right now, we're facing a threat... a powerful witch who's hunting us. We need help to stop him. And we hoped you might be willing to help us. Perhaps join a coven with us to defeat him." *Do I really need to go into my family history if they won't even consider helping us?* It was best to keep the details to a minimum. If he agreed, she would share the gruesome facts.

Rena pointed her finger at them and scowled. "And there it is. You're only here to get us to risk our lives for you. You're not here to know your possible family. You want to use us."

"Rena, hear them out."

"I just did."

"I don't expect you to care or to help us. This was Willow's idea. I thought it was a waste of time from the beginning." Justin grabbed Willow's hand. "Time to go. You asked. They answered."

"Wait a minute, son. I didn't answer anything. Of course I'll help you with whatever you need." Arthur turned to Willow. "What is it you need from me? My family has several witches. Some are stronger than others. Is it only earth powers you seek? I've got some distant cousins with air powers."

"Dad! You don't know what they're dragging you into."

Arthur didn't look Rena's way. He stared at Justin. "It doesn't matter. Justin is my son. I will always help him, no questions asked. The same way I'd help you or your brothers. It's what family does."

Justin's hand jerked in Willow's. It must be so hard for him to believe—to trust.

"There's more you should know before you commit to anything." Willow closed her eyes for a moment. "This witch has killed before and will again. If you agree to help us, you need to know the risks involved."

"He killed my mother."

Arthur gaped at Justin. "Maria?"

Willow gripped Justin's hand between both of hers. "He's pursuing Justin too."

"Why? Why is he killing witches?" Rena rubbed her arms as if to ward off a chill, though the weather was warm.

"For their power. He takes it." Willow sidled closer to Justin. "There's something else you should know."

Justin squeezed her hand.

For encouragement? Or to stop me? Willow glanced up at him, and he shook his head slightly.

"It's all right. They deserve to know. We can't expect him to help us without knowing the full truth." Willow swallowed hard and glanced at the ground before meeting Arthur's gaze. *Will it change how he sees me?*

"The witch who's after us is my father."

Rena drew in a sharp breath and took a step back. Justin glared at her before turning to his father. He wrapped his arm around Willow and anchored her to his side. Willow leaned against him, thankful for his support. It was a miracle he didn't blame her for what her family had done. Most would.

"The Immortal One is your father?" Arthur's voice was low but strong.

"You know him?" Justin pushed Willow behind him. "How?"

Does he suspect Arthur's a cohort of my father's? It was possible but doubtful. Edward occasionally hired mercenaries and other witches. She'd met none of them. He kept her and others segregated and only shared what they needed to know to complete whatever mission he had for them.

Arthur didn't strike her as the mercenary type, but there was no way to be sure. *Will we always have to mistrust everyone?*

Willow tried to step out from behind Justin, but he would have none of it. He kept a hand on her arm and shifted in front of her every time she tried to move around him.

"Justin, stop trying to protect me. I appreciate it, but I'm not in any danger. I doubt Arthur is one of Edward's accomplices. Nor do I need you to protect me from everything." *Will the men in my life always see me as weak and in need of protection? Will I always be a liability?*

"Willow isn't in any danger from me," Arthur said. "I would never harm her."

"Explain how you know Edward Marks." Justin tilted his head slightly toward Willow. "He doesn't have to be an accomplice to feed your father information in exchange for protection or something."

Valid point. Willow chewed her lip. That was a distinct possibility —her father having an informant, not that Arthur would be one.

"Is that his name?" Arthur shook his head slowly. "I've only ever heard rumors and whispers, ghost stories or tales told as warnings. I would never betray you or Willow. They call him the Immortal One, the one who comes in the dark to steal witches' powers or abduct them. If he comes for you, you're never seen again. That's all I know. It was a tale I heard as a child."

Great, I'm the daughter of a man people tell stories about to scare children. Sounded about right. He'd certainly terrified her when she was a child. As an adult, too, if she was honest.

Justin stopped trying to hold her behind him, and she stepped next to him.

Rena stared at her like she was a strange creature she couldn't figure out.

"If a witch is powerful enough, he covets their abilities for his own," Willow said. "If they're female, he might abduct them and attempt to impregnate them to create powerful children he can control and use for his twisted plans. I'm not sure what happened with Maria. Justin said she wasn't a powerful witch. If Edward planned to abduct her instead, maybe something went wrong. I don't know. Maybe it was just a coincidence and he wasn't who murdered her."

"He was. I know it. As soon as you told me about him, I knew it."

She wasn't about to argue with Justin. Her father could very well have been responsible. He was guilty of plenty else.

"Is that what he did with you? Impregnated your mother to get you?" Rena asked.

"Yes."

"How do we know you're not working for him? Helping him? Luring us into some trap so he can steal our powers? How does he steal powers from a witch?"

"She's not. He's hunting her too."

"Did she tell you that?"

Justin shot his sister a dangerous look.

Willow put a placating hand on his arm. "It's okay, Justin. You had your doubts, too, remember? It's completely understandable. I'd question it too. I don't know exactly how he steals their powers. He's never been forthcoming with any of the details. I know he needs an eclipse to work the spell. He's not able to take or keep their powers to wield himself. He takes the power to prolong his life. It's why they call him immortal. I don't even know how old he is. We're fairly sure he's at least a few hundred years old because of what a friend of ours learned from a vision an ancestor gave her." She rubbed her forehead with her palm. "The full truth is that I have helped him in the past. He used my magic to hunt witches. It was me who led him to Justin."

"You had no choice. And you didn't lead him to me. You misdirected him."

"He wouldn't have known about you if not for me."

"You were protecting your brother and yourself. I don't blame you."

Tears filled her eyes, but she willed them away. "I appreciate that, but it doesn't change the facts, and we can't expect them to help us without knowing all the pertinent information."

"I believe you, Willow, and I thank you for your honesty." Arthur put his hand on her shoulder and gave it a light squeeze. "I know it must be difficult to share such personal information. I don't know how much help I can provide, but I will do everything I can."

Rena sighed audibly. "If anyone is going to join some coven, it's me. I'm the more powerful witch, after all."

CHAPTER

TWENTY-EIGHT

Something dragged Justin from sleep. He lay still, sensing for danger. A soft mewling sound came from somewhere in the bedroom. He slit open his eyes and searched the hotel room's semidarkness. Shadows shrouded the space, but nothing moved.

He glanced at Willow beside him as the sound came again. She lay rigid. He sat up. Perspiration dotted her skin. Her fists clenched by her sides. Her body jerked slightly as her breath escaped in soft pants.

Is she having a vision? Should I try to wake her? During the last vision he'd witnessed, her eyes had been open. *Does that mean this is a nightmare? Or simply different from the last one?*

She'd needed water after the last one. He stalked into the bathroom to get her a drink in case she needed it. He set it on the nightstand next to her side of the bed. Tears leaked from her eyes and down her cheeks.

Son of a bitch! Vision or nightmare, he needed to wake her up.

"Willow, wake up, honey." He grasped her shoulders and shook her slightly.

She woke with a gasping breath and terror in her eyes. She stared blankly at him, as if she didn't recognize him.

Is she still caught in a vision?

"Willow? Honey? Are you all right? Are you with me?" He cupped her damp cheeks and searched her eyes.

A shaky sob shuddered through her, and she collapsed against him. He enfolded her in his arms. Crawling into his lap, she wrapped her arms around his neck as shivers and hiccupping sobs emanated from her.

Justin rocked her from side to side. He felt completely helpless about how to soothe her. He wished it was a physical enemy he could defend her against instead of whatever terror threatened her mind. Her weight settled against his chest. She sniffled and turned her head so the paleness of her cheek shone in the moonlight from the open curtains.

He'd learned the first night they spent together that Willow couldn't sleep in total darkness. *Could this have something to do with it?*

"Sorry." She wiped her cheeks and folded her hands in her lap.

Her soft whisper took a few seconds to register in his brain. "You have nothing to apologize for. Can you tell me about it? Was it a vision?" He nodded toward the glass of water on the nightstand. "I brought you water if you need it."

She cast a sad smile in his direction before she reached for the glass and drank. "Thank you. It helps, though it wasn't a vision. Just a nightmare."

Just a nightmare? "What was it about?" He rubbed her back and cuddled her slight frame to his chest.

She was silent so long, he thought she wouldn't answer. He didn't want to press. If she didn't want to talk about it, then he would leave it be.

"The house I grew up in was old with an old dumbwaiter. It was blocked off in most places... covered up by a new wall or, in the kitchen, it was behind the freezer. The attic was the only accessible opening." She sighed and leaned her head against him. "My siblings used to think it was amusing to stuff me in and lower it to the basement."

Son of a bitch!

"It was so dark and cramped. No one heard me scream. It was full of cobwebs, and it smelled. They would leave me down there for hours unless Sebastian came home. They never did it if he was home. He always somehow knew I was in distress and would find me and get me out. The last time they did it, Sebastian blasted a hole through the cement in the basement with a sledgehammer and tore every last piece of the dumbwaiter out and destroyed it."

Sebastian was an ass, but without a doubt, he loved and protected his sister. *Perhaps I could be a little more tolerant of her brother in the future, for Willow's sake.* "How old were you?"

"The last time? Twelve. Sebastian was already powerful. I think they were afraid of him even then."

Only twelve years old? "How old were you when they first put you in there?"

She shrugged. "I don't remember. The first time I have any real memory of being there was when Sebastian got a groundskeeper to pull me up. Basty's hands were bloody from trying to do it himself. He held me, and I remember the streaks of blood and dirt on my yellow dress. The dress had been a present for my third birthday."

Justin closed his eyes and rested his chin on top of her head. *Only three?* She'd been just a baby. "Didn't any caregivers watch out for you? You said your brother got a groundskeeper. Why didn't they tell someone?"

"Any household staff learned to keep their mouths shut or they didn't last long. The few employees who have been around for years turn blind eyes to what happens in that house. Either they don't care, or they're too scared to say anything. I don't know what happened to that groundskeeper, but I don't remember ever seeing him again. Father had a habit of getting rid of people who saw too much. He killed one of my nannies right in front of us when she tried to protect us from him."

Rage shrieked inside Justin, but he pushed it back. She didn't need his anger. She needed his comfort. There would be a time and a place for him to unleash his rage on those who had terrorized her.

"I'm damaged goods," she whispered. "So many have been harmed because of me."

He lifted her chin, but she fixed her gaze on his chest. "Willow, please look at me."

Her watery gaze slowly lifted.

"You're not responsible for what your family did. They're monsters."

"But I helped them. I found witches for him."

"You were a child. They tortured you. Sebastian told me some of what you endured. You didn't help them willingly. It's not on you. Nothing they have done is on you." He kissed her forehead and hugged her tightly.

"I wish I could forget it all." She tilted her head back and stared at him. "Justin, make me forget for a little while." She kissed him softly.

"Willow..."

She was upset. He didn't want to take advantage of her emotional state. And anger still coursed through his veins. It was all he could do to contain the power his magic wanted to unleash.

"Please." Her soft lips caressed his. Her hands framed his jaw, and her tongue delved inside his mouth. "Please."

Desire overrode the anger and curbed the power lashing at his skin. He returned her kiss. She straddled his lap, and he groaned. Justin gripped her hips as their tongues dueled in a passion-fueled dance. Want spiraled into need as she moved against him.

He slipped one hand beneath her pajama shorts and cupped her bottom while his other hand slid under her top to caress her breasts. She moaned into his mouth as she pressed into his palm. Her nails skimmed over his naked chest as her fingers trailed lower and lower.

His eyes closed when her fingers reached their destination and wrapped around him. The breath left his lungs in a whoosh that ended in a groan as her clever hands explored him.

Any last vestige of hesitation deserted him. He yanked her top over her head. Their lips, separated only for a second, melded together once again. He lifted her enough to jerk her shorts off while she tugged on his underwear. They scrambled back into position and both gasped as skin met skin.

He blindly searched for a condom on the nightstand while she wrapped her arms around his neck and devoured his mouth.

"Hurry," she whispered past his lips.

His fingers clenched over the package, and he ripped it open against her back. He momentarily forgot his purpose—and perhaps even his name—as her heat embraced him.

"Justin?"

"Mmm...?"

"Condom?"

He blinked open his eyes as conscious thought returned. *Right.* He finished opening and discarding the package. She bit her lip as she watched him put the condom on. He worried he might embarrass himself if he didn't look away from her. She was so sexy and gorgeous, she made him physically ache.

Once joined, their bodies moved as if they were one.

Ecstasy sparked at the bottom of his spine and raced up it as they found their climaxes together.

Willow melted against his chest and rested her cheek on his shoulder. Justin brushed her dampened hair off her forehead and gazed at her beautiful face. His heart clenched. He was beginning to think he might be the one in jeopardy of not leaving their relationship unscathed. He already cared far more about her than any other woman he'd ever been with.

"Wow! You look different. You're practically glowing. I don't know how to describe it, but you look so much more... alive since the last time I saw you. What's going on? Dare I ask if a certain traveling companion has something to do with the change?" Cory grinned at Willow from the phone screen.

Willow glanced over her shoulder to make sure Justin hadn't returned with their breakfast. She looked back at her phone and smiled. "Maybe." She winced and searched beyond Cory for listening ears.

Cory chuckled. "Don't worry. Finn and Sebastian are outside arguing about how to unload the car. To stop myself from braining anybody with something heavy, I decided to sneak inside and call you. When will you arrive to help me referee these two?"

Willow laughed. "We're leaving this morning, but I'm not sure if it will get better or worse. Justin and Sebastian tend to butt heads too."

"You do see the common denominator here, right?"

Willow snickered. "I know my brother can be a lot to handle sometimes, but he means well—usually."

"I'll have to take your word for it." Cory peeked behind her. "Okay, so while we're still alone, spill the details. Things have obviously progressed with Justin."

"Yes, but we're keeping it casual, enjoying each other while we can. He's worried about hurting me because he's not the relationship type. I've assured him I'm not looking for a commitment."

"Why the hell not?" Cory grimaced. "Well, unless you don't want one. But if you do, then you deserve one."

Willow chuckled. "I appreciate the support, but you and I both know the future is uncertain. I'm okay with our arrangement."

"As long as you're okay with it. I know what you're saying, but as Finn has reminded me, we can't stop living because we're worried about what might or might not be."

"I one hundred percent agree, but I also want to have one aspect of my life that I don't have to constantly worry about. Justin and I are on the same page."

"Okay, then. Enough said. I'll mind my own business and let you enjoy your relationship. Just know that I'm here if you need to talk."

"I appreciate it. I really do, and I'll probably take you up on the offer at some point, seeing as you're my only friend."

"I need to introduce you to Mel. Besides you, she's one of the few people on this planet I consider a friend. She's always given me brilliant advice and been there to talk me through my crazy times."

Willow smiled. "I'd like to meet her. It's great that you two have remained such good friends through everything. It must be nice to have someone in your life to not only rely on but to have as a sounding board when needed."

Cory laughed. "Well, I did try to push her away for her own protection, but she wouldn't let me."

"That's because she's a good friend. Obviously, you've arrived and met up with Sebastian, but did everything go well? Were there any problems?"

"Smooth sailing. How did your mission go? We've been incommunicado for security reasons, of course, so all I know is what your brother grumbled at me before he started arguing with Finn. He said you located Justin's family."

Willow filled Cory in on the highlights of the encounter. "So, the good news, besides Justin finding his family, is that we'll have some help. His sister, Rena, is joining us in a few days. She has to tie up some things before she can leave."

Justin still wasn't thrilled with her joining them, but Willow wasn't sure if it was because he still hadn't come to terms with having a family or if he wanted a relationship with them. If his father, stepmother, or brothers had anything to say about it, though, Justin wouldn't be getting rid of them anytime soon.

The door opened behind her, and Justin walked in. He smiled at her and held up the tray of coffees with a bag in the middle before he spotted the phone. He lowered the tray and tilted his head.

"Justin, meet Cory. She and Finn have arrived at Sebastian's."

Justin jerked his chin. "Hey."

"Hi there. Nice to finally put a face to the name."

"Same." Justin walked to the table and put down the tray.

Cory mouthed, "Wow, he's hot!" once he turned his back.

Willow blushed and nodded.

Justin handed her a coffee and placed a muffin on a napkin in front of her. "It's the cranberry and orange one you like."

She smiled at him. "Thank you."

Loud voices preceded a door opening and closing on the other end of the phone.

Finn walked on screen carrying a box overflowing with plants. He looked over his shoulder. "You do you, man."

Sebastian's voice came from off-screen. "You want to waste your time worrying about stupid plants when all our lives are in danger just proves my point. You don't belong here."

Cory sighed and rolled her eyes at the camera. "You've obviously forgotten that plants are my jam, Sebastian. How about we dump you in the middle of a desert and see how you do with no water?"

Sebastian stalked into view. He stopped abruptly when his gaze landed on the phone. "Hey, Willow. Everything okay?" His voice softened and lost its edge.

Finn's mouth dropped open, and he lowered the box to the floor. "It's like he's two entirely different people. Nice to see you, Willow. When are you arriving?"

Willow grinned. "Hi, Sebastian. Hi, Finn. We're leaving this morning. If everything goes well, we should be there late tonight."

"Good, because I'm not sure one of us will survive much longer without your presence." Finn glared at Sebastian.

"Think my sister will save you?"

"No, I think she might save you."

"Put a sock in it, boys, or you both might need saving from me!" Cory scowled at them.

Finn walked over and kissed her lips. "Sorry, princess."

Cory smiled at him as he sat next to her.

Justin simply raised his eyebrows at Willow as he sat to drink his coffee.

Sebastian walked over and stood behind them. He scowled briefly at Justin before nodding slightly. "Any issues?"

Justin shook his head.

Willow let out a breath. She was half afraid Justin would bring up her nightmare from the night before, but he would never do that in front of Cory and Finn. He didn't know them. She didn't want him sharing it with Sebastian privately either, though. Her brother was too hard on himself for not always being able to protect her. She hadn't managed to convince him that it wasn't his job. He'd been a child too.

"The eclipse is only a week away. What if we all hole up here and hide until it passes? Then we'll have more time to get stronger and work as a team."

They all glanced at Cory. Finn nodded. They'd probably come up with the plan together.

Sebastian folded his arms over his chest. "I'm sick of hiding."

"No one told you to stick around. Feel free to go up against your loving family on your own." Finn flung his arm toward the door.

Sebastian dropped his arms and cracked his neck to the side. He flicked a hand in Finn's direction. Finn paled and slumped in his chair.

Cory jumped to her feet and swung her arms in an arc. A blast of power emitted from her, sending Sebastian several feet across the room. "How dare you attack him with your water ninja spell? You bastard!"

"Sebastian, stop!" Willow dropped the phone as she stood.

Justin grabbed it and propped it against the tourist book the hotel kept in the room.

Sebastian lowered his hands and scowled at the phone. Finn stood and stumbled slightly, but he made it the few feet necessary to take a swing at Sebastian. Sebastian swerved, but Finn was ready for him and swung with his other arm and connected. Sebastian's face turned with the force of the blow. Finn wavered.

Cory grabbed his arm and threw her hand between them. "That's enough. Sebastian, you deserved that. Finn, you need to sit down and have some water to replenish what he took."

Sebastian rubbed his jaw and said nothing.

Cory maneuvered Finn to his chair then disappeared from view.

"As entertaining as this, if we can't stop fighting among ourselves, how are we ever going to stand together to fight the real enemy?" Justin leaned back in his chair with his arms crossed.

Cory returned with a bottle of water for Finn. "I like you already, Justin. It's a shame these two don't have your sense."

Finn chugged the entire bottle then grimaced at Sebastian. "I'm done. Are you?"

Sebastian gave him a quick nod.

Willow slid back into her chair and sipped her coffee. "I've been thinking. Miranda sensed me in my vision. What if we could somehow use that to misdirect them?"

Cory handed Finn a second bottle and leaned toward the phone. "How?"

"I'm not sure exactly, but maybe we could make them think we're somewhere we're not, or at least, not anymore. What if I tried to induce a vision of Miranda? I think I allowed her in because I was thinking of them. I could let her see a location then leave immediately after. That could buy us some time."

Justin frowned and shook his head. "It puts you at too much risk. I don't like it."

"Neither do I." Sebastian leaned on the back of an empty chair. "Besides, with the eclipse so close, they'll be getting desperate and more likely to make mistakes. That gives us the advantage."

Willow bit her lip. She knew they wouldn't like that plan, and if so they really wouldn't like her other idea. "True, which is why I had another thought. We could pick a place of our choosing, a place with water for Sebastian and lots of vegetation for Cory but remote enough so we won't draw attention and Justin will have the freedom to let loose with his powers and not worry about harming innocent bystanders. It could be a place with plenty of animals for Rena to call too. Somewhere that hinders Miles's powers would be a bonus. Once we're ready, I could try to lure them in with a vision that Miranda could pick up on again."

Cory looked over her shoulder. "We're not too far from the water, but it's populated here. The neighborhood's brimming with people."

"The point was to hide in plain sight." Sebastian stuffed his hands in his pockets. "I still don't like the danger it puts you in, but your idea does have merit. We could alert them a different way. I could use an old alias they're sure to be tracking. Or access a family bank account they monitor."

"They'll be suspicious if you make such a grievous error. My way, they'll think they have the upper hand. Now that I know what to look for, I'll know if she's peeking into my vision. I'm sure of it. In the past, I've always resisted the visions. Now, I'm learning to embrace them. I'll be open to them and able to concentrate if she shows up. I'll be in control, not her."

Justin took Willow's hand resting on her thigh and squeezed. It gave her the support she needed to continue.

"I think Justin's cabin might be the perfect place. It fuels all our powers, water, plants, animals. But the forest might make it harder for some of Miles's spells to work fully. It will provide a buffer at least." She looked at Justin. "Would that be okay with you? I hate to ruin your sanctuary."

"It's just a place." Justin rubbed his thumb soothingly over hers. "Besides, my cabin has the added benefit of already being set up. We don't need to waste time searching for another place. It's booby trapped."

"That's certainly a perk." Finn grinned. "I'd like to hear more about the traps. I might have some ideas to add."

Justin smirked. "We can do that. Are we all agreed, then?"

Cory and Finn nodded.

Sebastian looked away. "I still don't like Willow opening her mind to Miranda."

"I agree," Justin said. "They might be suspicious if you suddenly leaked your location, but they don't know me and will be less likely to question if I slip up. They've been searching for me anyway, right? Let them find me."

Willow's hand jerked in his. *It's my fault they're looking for him at all.*

His thumb continued to stroke hers.

"You should stick with the plan to meet up here. Once you arrive, we'll hash out the details. I'm not sold on the location. Revisiting a past hideout, somewhere we just left, is never a good idea." Sebastian looked at the suitcase in his hand then the box Finn had carried in. "By the time you arrive, we'll have come up with alternatives. If you're still set on California, we can discuss it."

Willow stared at the table. Justin's plan to leak his location was a good one. *But does no one trust me to follow through?* They said it was for her protection, and she wasn't exactly looking forward to allowing Miranda into her mind for any length of time. *So, why does it feel like they don't have faith in me? Are they worried Miranda will get more from me than I intend? Or do they think I'm not powerful enough to control my visions?*

She hadn't been able to in the past, so it didn't surprise her if Sebastian thought she couldn't handle it. Cory was her friend, though. *Does she have so little faith in me?* Maybe she hadn't given them any reason to believe in her abilities. Justin had seen her at her worst the previous night, terrified and helpless. It was no wonder he'd come up with an alternative.

"Willow?"

She lifted her head.

Cory stared at her with a curious smile. "Do you agree?"

"Sorry, my mind wandered. Agree to what?"

"To the plan. I know it was your idea to begin with, but with all the back-and-forth, I want to make sure we're all on the same page. I think Justin's idea is a good backup, but your idea of ensnaring Miranda with your vision is the smartest move. She'll be less suspicious."

Cory believes in me.

Willow glanced at Sebastian.

"I don't like it, but she's right. Miranda would never suspect you've become so powerful to lure them in with your visions. It's the perfect trap."

Sebastian thinks I'm powerful?

She turned her head and met Justin's gaze. "You agree as well?"

"I don't like it, either, but I know it's the soundest plan. If you don't want to, though..."

"No, I do. I'm in one hundred percent."

They didn't question her capabilities. She needed to stop doubting herself too. She knew she could do it. She wasn't afraid of her sister anymore. In fact, her nightmare reminded her that Miranda was long overdue for some payback.

THIRTY

"Having doubts?"

Willow glanced away from the window to Justin. "Doubts?"

"About the plan. You can back out at any time. I could reveal my location instead. Or we can change the strategy entirely and turn around. Just say the word."

She mustered a smile. "No, I'm not having doubts."

"Then what is it? You've been silent since we got on the road. Considering the dreary, rainy day, I don't think there's been much out that window to capture your attention for the past hour. Or is it the location that's bothering you? Your brother didn't completely rule out the cabin."

Willow spared a glance out the windshield. She hadn't even registered it was raining. *It wasn't when we left San Francisco, was it?* "No, it's not that. I still think it's our best hope, but I'm open to listening to anything they come up with once we get there. I guess I've just been lost in my thoughts."

"Care to share? If it's not about the plan, then what?" Justin switched lanes on the highway and increased the speed on the windshield wipers as the rain turned from a sprinkle to a heavy drum pelting the glass.

"About the past. Did you notice Cory's necklace?"

Justin frowned and shrugged. "It was big, right?"

She chuckled. "I suppose it's on the larger side. It's actually a brooch Cory put on a chain. It was her ancestor's, Josephine. Josephine was in a coven with my father centuries ago. He killed them all. Well, not Josephine. She escaped. I suppose it's possible others might have too. That's the thing. I've been trying to piece it together. What made him the way he is? Did he just snap one day, or had he planned it all along? It had to be premeditated to a certain degree because he had to figure out how to use another witch's power and he had to plot what he would do and how, right? According to Cory, Josephine fled England because members of their coven had gone missing and she sensed she and her unborn child were in danger. So it didn't happen all at once."

"Your father didn't talk about it? Didn't brag about how powerful he is? Let slip some details about how he got the drop on powerful witches?"

"Edward isn't much of a talker, and he's always been secretive. He watches everyone with his soulless eyes. The few stories I've heard him tell over the years had sparse details, and they changed to suit whatever point he wanted to make at the time." She rubbed the center of her forehead. "I'm not sure if he's a compulsive liar or just a manipulative one, maybe both." She rested her head against the back of the seat and closed her eyes. "I thought if I could unravel some of the lies, rumors, and suppositions from how it all started, that would help us defeat him once and for all."

"His power is fire, so isn't your brother the strongest way to combat him?"

"It's hard to explain. Sebastian is enormously powerful, the strongest water wielder I've ever seen or heard of. But on the rare occasion he tried to fight our father, it was almost like his power got diminished somehow. I think it's the abuse from our childhood. Maybe we've been conditioned not to fight back because the retaliation is always so much worse when we do."

"Edward is his father. Maybe he has some lingering hope that his father will change? I thought I would feel nothing for my father, but when I actually confronted him and found out I have a whole family I never knew about…" Justin shrugged. "Feelings are complicated."

"There's a stark difference between Edward and Arthur. Edward is no longer even human, if he ever was. Sebastian loathes him. No familial feelings or ties linger between them." She reached over and took Justin's hand. "I'm glad you admit you have feelings about your family, though. I think they're wonderful."

He smiled at her and intertwined their fingers before returning his attention to the road. "I'm not ready for regular family dinners or anything, but I'm not completely opposed to hanging out with one or two of them from time to time."

"It's a start." Willow turned her head and looked out the passenger window. Rivers of rain streamed across the glass. "When I was a child, Edward told a story about how glorious it was watching the plumes of smoke over the treetops from a neighbor's house as his childhood home burned to the ground. No one suspected he was responsible, and he cast the blame on someone else. He'd told it as an instructional tale to extoll the merits of infiltrating a group and exploiting their weaknesses while no one was the wiser. I don't know the details. If he gave them, I've forgotten or wasn't listening closely enough. He had beaten both Sebastian and me. The pain and the fear of what more he might do distracted me, but I remember fixating on the fact that he had watched it from such a distance that he could only see the smoke above the trees. How had he started the fire and kept it small enough for so long to visit a neighbor's house and be gone long enough that no one would suspect him? His power tends to be explosive, fireballs, not tiny flames, and he never seemed to have much control over the size or where it landed. I used to think he wasn't concerned with control. He liked the destruction. He liked the display of power."

"I'm not sure I follow. Are you saying Edward lacks control of his powers? Can we exploit that somehow? Can emotion trigger him like it does me?"

"He's never been very emotional, so I don't think that's it. And you've gotten much better at controlling your powers. I'm not really sure why the story is stuck in my head. It's like a thread I can't stop tugging on."

The hair on her arms raised. Cold seeped over her skin. She turned her head to alert Justin, but her vision faded, and a roaring filled her ears.

A smell surrounded her in the darkness. Smoke. There was no heat, only a heavy, cloying scent filling her nostrils. Sounds filtered in. Whispers. People were talking, but she couldn't make out their words. They were male voices. The blackness gradually lightened, and shapes took form like she was drifting out of a tunnel. Burned remnants of a structure scattered the ground in blackened clumps. Two men stood on a stone driveway beyond.

Willow sucked in a breath. Edward stood facing her. He was younger, probably around her age, but his eyes and nose were the same. *Could it be an ancestor instead?* No, she knew it was him. The man he spoke to turned, and Willow gasped. They were identical. Her father never mentioned any siblings, let alone a twin brother.

"Eddie, I don't know how it happened. I fell asleep, and when I woke, the house was on fire. I swear I didn't do it on purpose."

Edward patted him on the shoulder. "Of course not, but you must see how it looks to an uninformed observer. You fought with Father over the engagement, and now he's... gone. Someone set the fire intentionally, and you were the only one home. They'll arrest you, Theo. You need to leave before they do. The fire's bad enough, but if they find out you're a witch? You'll be executed on the spot."

Theo hung his head. "You're right. How could this have happened?" He buried his face in his hands. A sob shook his shoulders.

Edward smirked as he stared at the top of Theo's head.

Theo lifted it, and he straightened his shoulders. "Annabeth and I will leave for the Continent. We'll marry on the way."

Edward frowned. "Surely you must see that you would only endanger her. What if it happens again? I'm sorry, Theo, but you must break the engagement and leave her behind. For her protection, of course."

Theo tilted his head back and stared at the sky. "How will I ever explain this to her? She has no knowledge of witches."

"Perhaps I could tell her for you? It would be best if you leave immediately."

Theo stared at Edward for a moment before he nodded. "Yes, it's for the best. You'll use your magic? Make her understand? Perhaps you should make her forget about me all together. Can you do that?"

Willow shook her head. *His magic? His power's fire, not mind control, isn't it?*

Edward smiled. "Of course, Theo. You know I would do anything for you. I'll make sure she forgets."

Theo hugged him then stepped back and removed a ring from his finger. "You must return Annabeth's family ring to her." He dropped it into Edward's palm.

Willow recognized the ring. Her father never took it off. She'd always believed it was a family signet ring.

She shivered as an icy chill washed over her. The scene before her faded. All she saw were her father's soulless eyes staring over Theo's shoulder before darkness descended.

Justin whispered urgently in her ear, "Come back to me, Willow."

The scent and warmth of his skin seeped into her consciousness. The stubble on his jaw ruffled the hair on her forehead. The gap in his blue shirt revealed his tan chest and dark chest hair. She was in his lap. Willow tilted her head back.

Justin stared at her intently. "Thank God, you're back."

She clutched his arm and took in their surroundings. He must have pulled over when he noticed she was having a vision. The rain poured outside the Jeep like they were under a waterfall. Justin handed her a bottle of water, which she guzzled.

"He must've stolen his power," she whispered.

"What? Whose power? Who stole what?"

"My vision. I saw Edward. My father had a twin brother, Theo. Theo's power was fire. My father framed him for the house fire. I think Edward's power was—or is—mind control. It would explain so much. But how did he steal his brother's power? And why does he wear a signet ring from his brother's fiancée?" Willow sat up as her energy restored. She stared at Justin. "Could he have somehow locked Theo's power in the ring like Josephine locked her power in the brooch?"

"How can he wield another witch's power?"

"I don't know. He must've derived a spell. Maybe because he and Theo were twins. I know he's never been able to use another witch's power. He's tried too many times and failed."

"So, if we get the ring away from him, we'll have one less thing to worry about? He won't be able to wield fire against us."

"In theory, but now we know he has the power of mind control, and we have to figure out how to stop him from using it or influencing us." Willow shook her head. "I never understood why people, including me, would do his bidding. I would vow to resist whatever torture or manipulation he devised, but then, somehow, I would end up feeling so hopeless and comply."

"Might be why Sebastian was diminished against him too."

"Of course!" Willow clenched her fists in her lap. "There must be a way to stop him from influencing us."

"You should drink more water." Justin reached behind the seat for another bottle.

"I don't need it. I'm fine. In fact, I feel energized." She grabbed Justin's face and kissed him. "We have to call Sebastian, Cory, and

Finn. They need to know what we found out."

"What you found out."

She grinned. "I have hope, Justin. We can stop him. I know we can. We finally have a way to beat him for good."

THIRTY-ONE

"According to the GPS, we should be there in less than ten minutes." Justin glanced at Willow and back to the road.

She'd grown quieter the closer they got to Seattle. The call to Sebastian, Cory, and Finn to relay her vision of Edward and his twin had shocked them, especially Sebastian. His anger had pulsed around him like a hurricane. Justin had sensed it even over the phone.

Willow had talked him out of jumping on a plane to Connecticut to confront Edward on his own. Justin didn't relish the idea of anyone using mind control on him, either, but Sebastian had seemed particularly pissed off and out for revenge. If Finn and Cory hadn't been there to block him from walking out the door, Justin doubted Sebastian would have calmed down enough to listen to Willow as she convinced him that their plan was the best chance of success.

She gave a slight nod to acknowledge his statement, but her gaze was riveted on the darkening sky. They'd made good time, and night should still be an hour or so away. A storm must be rolling in.

A ping sounded off the roof, followed by several more. "What the…?" He leaned closer and peered out the windshield.

A cacophony of sounds erupted as hail pummeled against the Jeep. A car swerved into his lane. He threw out his arm to brace Willow as he slammed on the brakes. She gasped and stared out the window at the headlights of the car inches in front of them. Hail the size of golf balls pinged off the hood of the Jeep and thumped against the top of the car.

"Will it come through?" Willow searched the roof over their heads.

Justin glanced in the rearview mirror. They had just driven through an underpass. "Hold on."

He reversed and spun the Jeep around. Vehicles lined the residential street. Some hadn't even bothered to pull over, too shocked by the storm.

Justin stopped the Jeep beneath the underpass. At least it would provide protection until the storm passed. *Hailstorms don't last long, do they?*

Willow grabbed his arm with one hand and reached for her phone with the other. "We need to call Sebastian and Cory. It's Miles."

"What do you mean? Did you have another vision?"

She dialed, but no one answered.

"No. The storm. Miles is causing the storm!" She tossed her phone in her lap. "Go! We have to get to them. They're under attack. I know it!"

He didn't hesitate. Tires squealed as he stepped on the gas and made a U-turn. Cars littered the road like an obstacle course, but he sped around them.

Willow braced herself with one hand on the handle above the door and the other on the console between their seats. "Please hurry."

The hail stopped as abruptly as it started, and the sky cleared unnaturally fast.

Justin sped through a stop sign. Car horns honked as people came out of their stupors to navigate the roads as he barreled past.

"It should be just up ahead. Look for your brother's car."

"There!" Willow pointed to a brown house halfway up the street.

Justin searched but didn't see Sebastian's car. "How do you know? Do you see a house number?"

"No, but I see that."

He followed her finger with his gaze. A wave of water rose from a swimming pool next door to the brown house and surged into the backyard. He brought the Jeep skidding to a stop in front of the house. They both leaped out and ran around the side of the house.

Cory and another woman on the ground were drenched. Finn threw a punch as he jumped on the woman, who scrambled to get to her feet.

"Stay out of my head, bitch!" he shouted.

That must be Miranda. Her head whipped to the side as Finn's fist landed. She crumpled to the ground unconscious.

Finn stumbled over to Cory, who had managed to climb to her knees. A trail of blood divided the white skin of her forehead. Tendrils of her auburn hair coiled around her throat. Her blue eyes were glassy and dazed.

Sebastian faced a man who Justin could only assume was Miles. He had the same brown hair as Miranda, but his eyes resembled Sebastian's. Miles threw a blast of power that reverberated through the surrounding air. Sebastian blocked it and sent one of his own.

Justin reached deep inside himself and concentrated his magic on the earth beneath Miles's feet. The ground rumbled and fell away. Miles disappeared into the sink hole.

Sebastian yelled, "Bury him!"

Justin nodded, and the ground shook. The sink hole's walls collapsed.

Miles burst into view in a cloud of dust. He balanced in the air like a surfboarder riding a wave. Glaring at Justin, he jumped to the ground. "The earth mover, I presume." He glanced at Sebastian. "Gathering strays, brother?"

Miles swung his arm. A lash of wind hit Justin, lifted him up, and threw him against the side of the house. He fell to the ground and shook his head to right his senses. It was like being hit by a truck. His whole body ached.

Willow left Cory's side and ran toward Justin. Grabbing the side of the house, he dragged himself to his feet.

A bang ricocheted through the air, and a tree the height of a three-story building with a trunk as wide as his shoulders fell from the tree line edging the backyard. It could crush a house, let alone Miles, who stood underneath. Justin's gaze shot to Cory. Still on her knees, she had her arms raised and a fierce look of determination on her face. Miles threw up his hands. The tree kept falling but at a much slower pace.

Justin threw everything he had left at the ground beneath Miles. If he could knock Miles off balance and distract him, the tree could finish its job. The ground shifted, and Miles stumbled.

Sebastian walked slowly toward Miles, launching blasts of power. Miles fell sideways as the tree crashed to the ground. Branches cracked, broke, and fell away as the canopy collided with the earth. Miles screamed in pain as branches battered and skewered him. The wide trunk shuddered.

Sebastian ran closer, calling, "Finish him!"

"Stop!"

The screech brought Justin's head around. Miranda had her arm wrapped around Willow's throat with a knife pressed into her delicate skin.

"If he dies, so does she," Miranda hissed. Her gaze leaped from Sebastian to Justin to Cory.

Rage vibrated through Justin, and the ground shook. Blood trickled down Willow's neck as Miranda pressed the knife into her skin.

"Justin..." Sebastian growled as he lowered his arms and faced Miranda.

"That's right, brother dear. Tell your new pal I won't hesitate to kill worthless little Willow if you don't do what I say." A snarl curled her thin lips. Her beady black eyes darted between them.

Anger and power twisted inside Justin as fear coated his every thought. "Let. Her. Go."

Car alarms blared up and down the street. Glass shattered as windows fell from their frames. The ground heaved all around them. Cory stood with Finn's help. He held her in his arms as they stared at Willow and Miranda.

Justin struggled to control his power so Miranda didn't hurt Willow further.

Then Willow smiled at him.

What's she doing?

Her eyes pleaded with him, but he didn't know what she wanted him to do. Her smile and gaze felt like a warm caress. The ground stopped shaking and rumbling.

She dropped her hands from Miranda's arm around her throat. "Listen to me. Stop doing Father's bidding. You don't know who he really is."

"Shut up! I know exactly who he is." Miranda dragged Willow backward toward the tree and Miles.

"His power isn't fire. It's mind control. He stole his brother's power and killed him. His twin brother."

Miranda stopped, her gaze darting to Willow.

"I had a vision and saw it all."

The tree branches shook, and Miles climbed to his feet, one arm hanging uselessly at his side. Blood poured from wounds in his shoulder and thigh. "So what?" He climbed over a branch and grimaced as he clutched his leg.

"He'll kill you both too. You know it's true. He'll turn on you. That's what he does. Help us destroy him."

Miles glared at Willow.

Willow looked up at Miranda. "Read my mind. You'll see it's true."

Miranda frowned and lowered her arm slightly. Justin breathed a sigh of relief as the knife stopped cutting into Willow's skin.

Miranda looked at Miles. "She's telling the truth." Her head tilted. "He controls fire with his ring?"

Willow frowned but nodded slightly.

No doubt, she hadn't wanted to impart every detail to her sister's probing mind.

Miles glanced around the backyard at everyone. "What are you proposing?"

Sebastian kept his gaze on Miles. "A temporary alliance."

"Let her go, and we'll tell you the plan." Justin took a step forward, his hands fisting.

Miranda stared at Miles until he gave her a slight nod. She dropped her arms and backed away from Willow. Holding a hand to her throat, Willow ran to Justin. He caught her in his arms and faced her twisted siblings. Cory and Finn leaned heavily against one another as they edged closer to the house and away from them.

Sebastian stuffed his hands in his pants pockets like he was out for an evening stroll. "It's rather simple. Lure Edward to a place of our choosing, and work together to ambush him. If you can find a way to separate him from the ring, it would make exterminating him that much easier."

Night had fallen, but the lit house and streetlights amplified the moon's brightness, making it easier to see the backyard and its occupants. All around them, silence echoed, as if the world was holding its breath, waiting for a response.

Miles cast his gaze over them. Reaching his side, Miranda wrapped her arm around him to lend her support as his blood continued to flow, spreading a dark stain over his clothes.

How is he still standing? Will he even survive to help with our plan? Justin held Willow closer. *Wouldn't it be easier to take them out now, while they're weak?*

Willow patted his chest, and he glanced down at her. She shook her head slightly. Miranda stared at them. Justin blanked his mind and started rebuilding the engine of his Jeep in his head.

Miranda looked back at Miles.

"We'll be in touch." Miles leaned on his sister. "Miranda, toss Sebastian your phone."

She frowned but did as he requested. "The password is all sixes," she muttered as Miles put his good arm over her shoulders.

Together, they slowly walked to the front of the house. The closer they got, the heavier Miles leaned on his sister. Maybe nature would take its course and take out Miles as a threat.

Sebastian picked up Miranda's phone while he kept his gaze on his siblings.

"We should get out of here before anyone fixates on us." Finn swung Cory into his arms. "Now that the crazy weather and earthquakes have stopped, people will be coming out of hiding. We need to be long gone before they figure out this is the epicenter of the mess."

Cory's skin was pale, and she sagged against him.

Justin frowned. "How badly is she hurt?" *Does she need a hospital?*

Willow dropped her hand from Justin's chest. "She has a concussion. Finn said Miranda hit her over the head with a rock before we got here."

Sebastian fell in beside them as they made their way to the front of the house.

Justin kept an eye out in case Miles and Miranda had decided to double-cross them. A vehicle sped off down the street.

Willow sighed heavily. "They're gone."

"You're sure?" Justin took her hand in his.

She nodded and gave him a squeeze. He stared at the blood crusting on her skin. Anger and fear for her rose inside him once again. She could have died. Her thumb stroked over his palm.

Finn put Cory in the passenger seat of a sports car. He glanced at them as he rounded the front of the car. "I'm taking her to the closest hospital to get checked out." He jerked his head toward the house. "Can I count on you three to handle our things?"

"Of course."

Finn nodded at Willow, got into the car, and drove away.

Sebastian sighed. "Looks like I'll be riding with you."

Justin followed his gaze to the street. A telephone pole lay on Sebastian's car. The roof was crushed—the car wouldn't be going anywhere.

Should be a real fun trip.

CHAPTER
THIRTY-TWO

Willow leaned against the window frame and watched Sebastian pace back and forth across the front lawn of Justin's cabin. Anger still radiated from him. He wasn't dealing with the news about Edward well. His hatred for their father consumed him. She worried that it would blind him if and when it came to a confrontation.

Can he see past his anger and think rationally?

The ride down from Seattle had been tense. Sebastian had alternated between wanting to jump on a plane and surprise Edward, Miles, and Miranda with an attack and lure them into an ambush. He didn't trust their siblings any more than he trusted their father. He'd gotten Miles's current phone number from Miranda's phone then tossed it out the window before they'd even left Seattle. He didn't trust Miles not to track the phone and betray them. He'd texted the number from a burner phone so Miles could reach them if he and Miranda did decide to help.

Willow didn't trust her siblings, either, but she at least allowed for the possibility of their survival instincts to prevail over any loyalty to their father. They had to see that Edward would eventually betray them all.

She'd tried, with limited success, to get Sebastian to concentrate on spells and counterattacks to Edward's mind control. Hopefully, that was what had him so preoccupied.

Justin had disappeared into the woods to set traps once again. At first, Sebastian had assisted, but they'd inevitably ended up arguing over the right way to do something. Justin had told him to stay near the cabin for the sake of both their sanity. Surprisingly, Sebastian had complied.

Willow sighed. She didn't know how to help him. Finding out about Edward hadn't made her react the same way. She saw it as a possible means to stop him once and for all. They had more information. Knowledge was their weapon.

Cory and Finn should arrive soon. Perhaps they would have some advice. Thankfully, Cory had gotten a clean bill of health. She'd escaped with only a slight concussion and had insisted she felt fine. She was more concerned that Miranda had found them through her parents. Cory felt guilty, but as Willow had assured her, it wasn't her fault.

Miranda had plucked their location from Cory's parents' minds. There was no way she could've known that a video call with her parents could lead Miranda to her. She'd been careful not to divulge anything and had used an untraceable number. They'd taken every precaution, but a visible license plate from a car parked on the street had been all Miranda had needed.

Willow frowned. She was the one who had underestimated Miranda's abilities. She should've known and warned everyone.

Sebastian abruptly stopped and threw his hands out to the sides. Willow felt the vibration of power in the air as droplets of water rose all around him. The drops collided and formed streams of water that moved faster and faster until a tornado of water whipped around her brother, obscuring him from view.

What is he doing? Willow ran to the door and yanked it open.

The tornado of water rose over Sebastian. He flung his arms, and it swirled across the ground before smashing into the small shed. The whistling was followed by a roar, and the vortex of water obliterated the shed and its contents. Shards of wood pierced the wet ground. The upside-down lawnmower's wheels spun in the air. The handle was bent and driven into the ground.

Sebastian fell to his knees, drained.

Willow ran back inside and grabbed as many bottles of water as she could carry. She dropped to her knees next to her brother and handed him one. "Drink."

He did, guzzling it down before sitting back and resting his arms on his drawn knees. "Thanks."

"That was impressive."

"Anger has its uses if you can channel it properly."

She scooted next to him and leaned against his arm. "I'm worried they could use your anger against you if you're not careful."

"I know. I'm trying to keep it in check."

"Do you remember when we were little how you taught me to build a special garden in my mind? A place where I'd always be safe and nothing could hurt me?" The garden had grown from a small little plot of flowers to a parklike space full of trees, meandering paths, ponds, bridges, and benches surrounded by bursts of color. She'd built it in her mind and expanded on it every time she'd needed an escape from reality.

He nodded once.

"I've been thinking about how to keep Edward and Miranda out of our heads. I surrounded my garden with a tall brick wall. We need to employ a similar process around our minds—envision a wall they can't penetrate."

She'd built the brick wall around it the first time Miranda had gotten into her mind, seen the garden, and threatened to set it on fire with Willow inside.

"Letting Miranda enter my mind and see exactly what I think of her and all the ways I've envisioned killing her has always been an effective deterrent for me."

Willow frowned. "That may work with Miranda, but I doubt it has any effect on Edward."

Sebastian turned his head and stared into the trees. "He used fear to control us."

"Of course he did." He used their love for one another and fear of pain and torture.

"I don't mean the torture. I think he manipulated our thoughts and amplified the fear—made us feel terror and made us doubt ourselves."

Willow nodded and rested her head on his shoulder. "I think so too. I used to think that his abuse had indoctrinated us to be terrified of him. Whenever he was present, my fear and insecurities were unbearable. Now, I think he made us feel that way intentionally so we wouldn't fight back."

"At times, I would freeze in place with terror, and I couldn't make myself move, no matter what I tried. I couldn't fathom why I was so weak around him."

"You weren't weak, Basty. You were never weak. Your strength saved us."

"I should've seen past his manipulations. He was always scheming. Everything was a game to him. I should've figured out his actual power. He never wielded fire except in rare situations. If fire was his real power, he would've used it more, like I wield water."

"Hindsight is twenty-twenty for a reason. None of us ever guessed. He's an expert manipulator." She lifted her head. "But now we have the advantage. We know the truth and can use it against him. Even if Miles and Miranda don't help us, we're still stronger now."

"Don't trust them, Willy." He stared into her eyes. "Promise me."

"I won't, but I can still hope they'll see that he has to be stopped and help us."

"Their selfishness might be enough to override their fear of him, but I only give it fifty-fifty odds."

They sat in silence for a long time.

Sebastian drank another bottle of water. "I think we can derive a spell to create your wall and keep them out. When Cory arrives, we can brainstorm something that works for each of us. It will be hard to keep visualizing a wall if we're battling."

Willow took a deep breath of relief. He was back to planning for the coming battle.

"You're right. Maybe we should tweak the spell to each of our strengths too. Like a wall of thorny vines for Cory, a towering enclosure of rock for Justin, and a whirlpool of deadly rapids for you."

"It will have to be sustainable and strong enough to last while we use our powers to battle and wield other spells."

"I'm confident we can come up with something together." She looked at the devastation of the shed. "I'm less confident that you can come up with a good explanation for Justin as to why you destroyed his shed."

Sebastian snorted. "He'll get over it."

THIRTY-THREE

The fire crackled and warmed the night air around them. Justin stared into the flames. It was a good thing the caretakers had mowed the lawn recently and he'd told them he would be around to handle the maintenance himself for a while because he could come up with no plausible explanation for the obliterated shed and everything inside it.

He scowled at Sebastian across the firepit. "You owe me a new lawnmower."

Sebastian gave him a bland stare.

Willow rubbed Justin's arm and scooted closer on the log bench. "Sebastian will replace the shed and everything that was in it. Won't you, Sebastian?"

"Will I?" Sebastian took a sip of his beer.

"Basty…"

Her brother rolled his eyes. "Fine."

Finn chuckled and shook his head as he took a sip of his own beer. Cory snuggled under his arm. They'd arrived about an hour before dinner.

Justin had worried where he would put everyone to sleep, but

Finn and Cory had set up a tent just outside the circle of benches surrounding the firepit. Sebastian had delivered a jab about sleeping under the same roof as the man sharing a bed with his sister, so Justin had gone inside, grabbed his own tent, tossed it at her brother, and told him he wouldn't have to. Sebastian had muttered something about preferring to sleep under the stars rather than endure Justin's lack of hospitality and set up the tent.

Willow snuggled closer, and Justin put his arm around her. "Cold?"

"Not anymore."

They were playing a waiting game. After dinner, they'd formulated a loose plan they could adjust to include or exclude the evil twins. Personally, he didn't trust them to do anything except betray them, but he'd been surprised before.

He gazed down at the top of Willow's blond head nestled against him. She had definitely thrown him for a loop more than once. She was stronger and braver than he would have ever given her credit for when they'd first met—more so than even she gave herself credit for.

Willow was gentle and kind but fierce when it came to protecting those she cared for. She didn't back down from a fight. She might not wield power the same as he, her brother, or Cory, but she still raced to put herself between them and her evil siblings.

His heart had literally stopped when Miranda had held the knife to Willow's throat.

"Justin, when is your family arriving?"

He glanced at Cory. "Rena's taking an early flight. She'll be here first thing in the morning. The rest who are coming will arrive by noon." He still couldn't believe they were coming. It seemed like some far-fetched tale or a prank that he had people ready to stand beside him. His father, stepmother, and brothers called every day just to say hello and check in. Rena had sent him one text—that day —with the date and time of her flight and to ask for directions.

Willow rested her hand on his leg. "It will be nice to see them, even under these circumstances. They're like the quintessential loving family I've only ever read about or seen on television."

Sebastian scoffed. "That doesn't exist. Everyone has skeletons in their closets. They may not have as many as our family, but I bet they're there somewhere."

Finn snorted. "As cheerful and trusting as always, Sebastian."

"No family is perfect, but it doesn't mean they're hiding dreadful things. My family is certainly not perfect. My parents have no idea I'm a witch, and I doubt they could grasp it if I told them." Cory sat up and took a sip from the glass of soda beside her. "We don't always see eye to eye, but I know they love me."

"Of course I know they're not perfect. I'm just saying it's clear how important family is to them, and they love each other. I've never witnessed that in real life." Willow smiled at Justin. "I'm glad Justin found them."

"Thanks to you." He kissed her forehead.

She shrugged. "I helped."

"Without your visions, it never would've been possible. Don't sell yourself short."

Cory angled her glass toward Willow. "Your visions have given us invaluable advantages. We'd be fighting Edward in completely the wrong way without them. Now we've crafted spells that will give us a real chance."

Justin rubbed Willow's arm as she blushed over the praise. He wasn't as confident about wielding spells as Sebastian, Cory, or Willow, but he hoped the spell would keep Edward out of his head long enough for him to do some damage.

A phone vibrated. Sebastian pulled it from his pants pocket and stared at the screen with a grimace. "It's Miles." He touched a button and held it out so they all could hear.

"It has to be tomorrow. Give me the coordinates."

Sebastian gazed at them.

They'd already discussed that it would be the next day or nothing. If Miles didn't call, then the eclipse would pass without a confrontation. But they had gambled on Edward needing the eclipse to extend the magic keeping him alive.

They all nodded, and Sebastian recited the coordinates. He disconnected the phone without saying another word.

Finn sighed heavily. "Well, that's that. It's on."

Cory leaned against him once again. "On one hand, I want this to be over, but on the other, I kind of hoped Miles wouldn't call and we'd have more time."

"If Miles didn't call, it would have meant his injuries were more extensive than we thought and he was dead." Sebastian rolled the bottle between his palms. "Whether he plans to betray us or not, he was still going to call. He may have told Edward everything, and they're setting a trap of their own. Or he and Miranda realize they're better off without Edward, and they're willing to set him up just enough to get him here. It doesn't mean they'll fight alongside us. Most likely, they'll keep their options open and wait to see which way the fight goes. We still need to come up with a plan to get that ring away from Edward, or we'll be fighting both his mind control and fire. Hopefully, Miles and Miranda will pull their punches until they decide which side to be on."

"He's right." Willow tugged on the blanket around her shoulders. "And even if they've decided to be on our side, if the fight isn't going in our favor, they will switch. Don't ever turn your backs to them."

THIRTY-FOUR

Willow stiffened. Her intuition told her something was happening.

"It's begun." Justin looked up from the tablet in his hands. Since the previous night, he'd been monitoring the cameras he'd placed around his property. No one had put it past Edward or Miles and Miranda to launch a sneak attack the day before. "Men in camouflage are approaching through the woods."

"We knew Edward would likely hire mercenaries. He's done it before in extreme situations, and he's desperate to get the power he needs to stay alive." Sebastian shrugged. "He's following a predictable pattern. There will be low-level witches too."

"The traps will weed out a bunch but not all." Justin swiped his screen and studied the cameras.

Sebastian looked at Cory. "Finn better be as good a shot as he claimed. If he can even get shots off in that weird tree capsule you made for him."

She glared at Sebastian before rolling her eyes. "He can. The plants are there to protect and conceal him."

Willow forced a smile to help lighten the tension permeating the room. "They'd have to chop the tree down to get to him, if they ever locate him." Last night during their strategy session, Finn had produced some sort of sniper rifle that one of his military buddies had procured for him. He was determined to level the playing field for them as much as possible. When Cory had sketched her plan and worked out the spells, Willow had been amazed. Finn sat in an egg-shaped capsule made of plants. The contraption was way up high in the branches of a massive redwood.

"Actually they'd have to chop a lot of trees down to reach the center one he's hiding in. I spelled an entire cluster." Cory turned her head to look at Rena and Arthur leaning against the wall. "Your family is protected out there too."

Justin's extended family had arrived. Not all were witches. Many had brought weapons of their own and were in the forest with Finn.

Arthur smiled at Cory and walked over to Justin. "I think that's our cue to take our positions." He placed his hands on Justin's shoulders. "Be careful, son."

Justin nodded. "You, too." He didn't flinch or back away from the contact. He was making progress in accepting his family. He'd even endured the awkward hug from his new family members that morning when they'd arrived.

Rena walked past him with a nod, which he returned. They still needed some work, but it was an improvement.

Willow nibbled on her lip. Arthur and Rena were to remain hidden as long as possible while sending animal helpers to assist. They were one of many levels of surprises the group had in store for her family. "Remember to block your minds from being read or influenced."

They both glanced at her and nodded before walking out the door.

To prevent Miranda from learning their entire plan, they had decided none of them would know everything. They had broken off into pairs for various stages of the plan, and each individual had come up with their own strategy for certain tasks as one more level of security.

Cory stood and rubbed her palms down the jeans covering her thighs. "It's go time, folks." She hugged Willow and fist-bumped Justin, then jerked her chin toward Sebastian before walking outside.

Sebastian walked over and grasped Willow's arms. "I wish you'd reconsider and stay inside the cabin. I don't want to worry about your safety and where you are."

"We talked about this, Basty." She would be in the woods in charge of alerting them to Edward's arrival and of any information she could provide on the witches he'd brought with him. She should at least be able to tell them how many, what power they had, and how strong they were. "Besides, the cabin could be leveled by fire or a tornado or something." She glanced at Justin. "Hopefully not, but it's a possibility."

Sebastian sighed heavily.

"You need to focus on your role, not me. Don't let your concern for me give them an advantage. I can do this."

He gave her a tight hug. "I know you can. It's not from a lack of faith in your abilities. You just happen to be the only one on this planet I give a damn about."

She hugged him back. "I love you. We're finally going to be free. We can end this today. Focus on that. You're stronger than all of them."

Sebastian kissed her on the forehead and nodded at Justin before disappearing out the door.

Justin handed her the tablet. "Remember how this works? You'll be able to see from all angles."

She nodded. "I've got this." He'd had her show him multiple times the previous night and that morning. Even through the cameras, she could tell by their auras if a witch approached. They'd tested it repeatedly.

Justin cupped her face in his hands and kissed her. "If this goes south, run. Don't try to play hero. Promise me."

Like that'll ever happen. She kissed him back. "We're going to win. I feel it."

"Willow..."

"Justin, I could no sooner leave any of you behind than I could suddenly sprout wings and fly, but I'll completely understand if you need to run."

He frowned and gave her an incredulous look.

"How is it any different?" she asked. "You expect me to run but not you? I may not have your power, but that doesn't make me a coward or mean I'll put my life before any of yours."

"You have plenty of power. That has nothing to do with it. And saving yourself instead of staying with no hope of survival doesn't make you a coward." Justin rested his forehead against hers. "I want to know you'll be safe no matter how this goes."

Knock, knock, Miranda's chiding voice echoed in her head.

"They're here." Willow swiped the screen until she saw the camera aimed at the dirt parking lot. Edward, Miles, and Miranda nonchalantly exited a black SUV like they were there for a friendly visit.

Justin gave her a swift kiss before leaving through the front door. She went out the back and signaled everyone to confirm their arrival. They'd come up with the idea to use old-fashioned pagers instead of cell phones or any other current form of more hackable technology. Most people didn't think about pagers anymore and, therefore, wouldn't think to search for the network. They'd also produced their own shorthand code words in case someone did get ahold of a pager during battle.

Sending up a prayer for their success, she crawled into the makeshift fort Justin had made for her just beyond the tree line. Someone could walk right by, or even over her if they climbed the fallen redwood, and never notice her. She would hear and see them, however, on the cameras.

Miles and Miranda led the way down the path. Edward always

put someone ahead of him to take the brunt of an attack. A male witch she didn't recognize followed Edward—to protect his back.

Willow studied the aura of the unknown witch—fire and not terribly high in power or experience if his darting gaze was any indication. She signaled the group.

Her eyes landed back on Edward. He had to be weakened, but it didn't show on his stonelike visage or in his strong gait. He no longer used a cane.

Did he find another way to gain power other than through the eclipse?

No. Otherwise, why would he risk coming here? He might've sent Miles and Miranda and the others, but he wouldn't risk himself unless he needed to. He needed to drain a powerful witch of their power to sustain his life. It was the only reason he would show himself. He must've cast a temporary spell.

Willow and Sebastian shared Edward's nose. She liked to think that was where the similarity ended. She felt nothing for him as she watched him on camera. He'd never been what a father should be to her.

Willow closed her eyes and refocused her thoughts. She fed as much power as she could into keeping her mind's walls intact to keep Edward and Miranda out.

She did a quick search through the cameras. A dozen or more mercenaries were dead or incapacitated from the traps. She paused on one screen.

Another witch approached through the woods—earth-based power, low level. She sent the information and direction. A ping echoed through the woods, followed by another louder report from a gunshot.

"Hello, brother."

Willow turned her head but couldn't see where Miles's voice originated. He had to be in front of the cabin where the path ended—unless he had cut through the woods.

The cameras. How could I forget the cameras? If the sound of Miles's voice is enough to rattle me, how will I keep my cool to be of any help?

Sebastian stood in front of the cabin with his hands in his pockets, as if he didn't have a care in the world. Miles stood before him, wearing an arrogant smirk.

A witch must've healed him. *How else could he appear unscathed from our last encounter? Where did our father find a healer?* That must also be how he walked without a cane. He'd had her search for one in the past, but it hadn't worked—not that she'd wanted to help him, anyway.

Miranda leaned against a tree off the path. Her head tilted from side to side. No doubt she was searching for minds to hack.

Edward stood at the end of the path. "You're such a disappointment, Sebastian. You could have been great. Instead, you let a piece of ass and your useless sister lead you astray."

His ravaged voice sounded like something straight out of a horror film. She'd always thought age had damaged his vocal cords, but maybe fire had burned them. *A price to pay for wielding his brother's power? Or maybe Theo had enacted some revenge before Edward stole his power.*

Willow frowned. *Does he think Sebastian's romantically involved with Cory?* Edward *had* instructed Sebastian to seduce her. *Is that what he thought happened? How could he not know about Finn? Did Miles and Miranda not tell him?* She shook her head. It didn't matter —just like him calling her useless didn't matter. She was more than used to it. She knew it wasn't true, at least not anymore.

Sebastian said nothing.

That's right, Basty. Don't let him get into your head.

Willow split the viewing screen and searched the other cameras while keeping the one with the front of the cabin on the screen. *Where did that fire witch go?*

"Where is the little plant wielder? Have you taught her how to do more than grow some vines?" Edward flicked his gaze at Miles.

Miles wandered around the side of the cabin, presumably to search for Cory.

"Your brother and sister tell me you have an earth wielder in your little group now. Has he abandoned you already, or is he just too scared to make an appearance?"

"Come out, come out, wherever you are." Miles's singsong voice came from less than twenty feet in front of Willow's hiding place.

Cory could be anywhere. They had intentionally not shared their hiding spots. She must be within sight of the cabin, though, so she could probably hear them fine.

There you are. The fire witch approached the cabin from the south. He must've circled around while Willow searched the other cameras. She would have to be more diligent about scanning through them. Willow sent out his location.

Something whistled through the air behind her. She turned her head in reaction before scrolling through the cameras for the source. An arrow protruded from a mercenary. Two of Justin's uncles had arrived with bows. Miles had stopped in front of where she hid and stared into the woods behind her.

That's right, brother. We're not alone.

He searched the area then continued on.

"Come now, Sebastian. You can't possibly intend to face me alone. Why don't you call your little friends out of the woods, and let's get started, shall we?" A flame ignited in Edward's palm.

Vines wrapped around the fire witch in the woods. He let out a muffled screech before his mouth was covered, and he was spun up like a fly captured in a spider's web.

Willow smiled. *Way to go, Cory.*

Miranda stalked toward the sound then stopped. She looked back and shook her head at Edward. He didn't react but rather stared intently at Sebastian.

Is he trying to get into Sebastian's head?

Muffled gunshots and the occasional scream echoed from the woods.

Miles made a full circle around the cabin and arrived back at the front.

The flame in Edward's hand grew into a ball of fire. He launched it at Sebastian. Sebastian met it with a torpedo of water. The two elements collided in midair and canceled each other out. A brief look of surprise crossed Edward's face. He must not have thought Sebastian could fight back. He never had before.

His mind control isn't working. Sebastian's block held.

Miles sent a wave of power barreling into Sebastian, knocking him to the ground.

Willow stifled a gasp. *Miles isn't pulling his punches. He isn't on our side.*

Willow strengthened her resolve. At least they knew for sure.

The ground shot up beneath Miles's feet and sent him flying through the air. He landed a few feet from Edward.

Justin!

Miranda ran to Miles. Edward didn't spare either of them a glance. He sent wave after wave of power at Sebastian as her brother climbed to his feet.

Sebastian threw up his hands with a block, but the unrelenting blasts of power caused him to stumble. He braced with his legs apart and grimaced. He wouldn't be able to hold out for long.

Justin and Cory walked out of the forest, blasting Edward from either side. He retreated a few steps before sending another fireball in each of their directions. Cory let out a cry as the fire broke through her block. Flames licked up her arms. Sebastian sent a torrent of water and doused the flames. Smoke drifted up from her tattered shirt.

Miles battled Justin on the other side as they traded blasts of power. The opposing earth witch appeared behind Cory. Willow moved to call out a warning, but Cory swung around and blasted the witch before she could. He stumbled back. Edward battled Sebastian. They were holding their own, but they were far from winning.

I have to do something.

Willow searched the cameras. *Where's Miranda? What is she up to?* No more mercenaries sneaked up on them as far as she could see.

It was time for another surprise. She signaled Arthur and Rena.

Something crashed through the woods—a lot of somethings. A herd of deer galloped through the clearing. The witches all scrambled to get clear. Cory used the surprise to skewer the earth witch with a branch. He hung by it from where it lodged into a tree. Red covered his chest and abdomen.

A flock of geese descended and dive-bombed Edward and Miles, who dove for cover.

Sebastian guzzled water from one of the bottles he'd stashed around the property while Justin crouched low to the ground with his fingers buried in the dirt. His chest heaved from exertion. Cory leaned against a tree with her hands on her knees.

Edward raised his hand with a fireball.

Miranda stepped out from behind a tree behind him with her arms raised. She held an ax. Slicing it through the air, she severed his hand from his body. The fireball extinguished as the hand with the signet ring flopped to the ground. He bellowed in agony and swung around. Miranda stumbled backward, tripping and falling to the ground. Edward raised his good arm while blood poured from the other.

Blasts of power hit him from all sides as Sebastian, Justin, Cory, and Miles attacked him together. Willow dropped the tablet and scrambled from her hiding place. She would add what power she could. Rena and Arthur joined her as she ran to the front of the cabin.

Edward fell to the ground as they stood around him, united, joining their magic. Their power pummeled him. He aged before their eyes. His hair turned white and receded. His frame diminished, and his clothes hung. His skin turned sallow and spotted. Shock and fear etched his features before they crumbled away.

Nothing but dust remained in his pile of clothes.

CHAPTER

CHAPTER
THIRTY-FIVE

A large circle of people and witches stood around Edward's remains in stunned silence. They'd exited the woods one by one to join the group. Finn and Cory held each other close. Arthur stood with his arm around Rena and the rest of his family at his back. Sebastian, Miles, and Miranda all stood with their gazes fixed on the ground.

Willow slipped her hand into Justin's as she stared at what was left of the man—no, not a man, the pure evil—that had terrorized them and others for centuries. She felt nothing but relief. That wasn't her father. She'd never had a father.

She raised her gaze to Sebastian, who looked across the circle at Miles and Miranda standing together. They'd come through.

Did they plan to all along, or did they decide to switch sides in the midst of battle? Did it matter?

Without Miranda striking the blow that removed Edward's control over his twin's stolen power, they might not have been able to defeat him. Not even their reasons mattered at that point.

Miles kicked at the pile of clothes. A small cloud of dust rose and floated away on the wind.

Is he worried Edward will somehow come back from that?

With a flick of his wrist, he sent the air above the remains swirling. The clothes and powder rose within the torrent of wind. It hovered above them before the clothes shredded to nothing and the powder dispersed in every direction, carried far away on the wind Miles wielded. When nothing remained, Miles dropped his arms and stepped out of the circle.

"Bargain met, brother." He stared at Sebastian.

Sebastian nodded.

Miles turned and walked down the path, Miranda following.

Will I ever see them again? Do I even want to?

They hadn't even spared her a glance. They may have helped defeat Edward, but she had endured years of torture at their hands. They were no more her siblings than Edward had been her father. Sebastian was her only family.

Justin squeezed her hand. "Are you okay?"

She gave him the best smile she could muster. "I'm fantastic. I'm finally free."

He smiled and hugged her.

She rested her head against his chest. *What will become of us now?* She doubted he would want to stay at the cabin. *Where will he go? To San Francisco to get to know his family? Will he ask me to go with him?* Willow glanced up at his face.

He stared around his property.

Is he cataloging the wreckage? Already saying goodbye to this sentimental piece of land?

Cory and Finn went inside the cabin.

Arthur clapped Justin on the shoulder, and Willow stepped back to give them some room. She glanced around at the dozen or so people milling about. They would all have to be fed.

Sebastian stood at the edge of the yard staring down the path.

Walking over, she bumped his arm with hers. "Penny for your thoughts?"

Sebastian looked down at her. "They took the ring."

She searched the ground behind her where the hand had fallen then down the path. "What for? You don't think they can wield it like Edward could, do you?"

"Only time will tell."

THIRTY-SIX

"What will you do now?" Cory's eyes were red rimmed from all the crying she'd done. She hadn't handled taking a life well, despite all her assurances that it had been a choice between her life or the unknown witch's. She'd done a healing spell on the tree branch that had killed the witch, so only a slight indentation remained.

Willow glanced around the empty cabin. Justin's family had dispersed that morning, after ensuring no trace of the battle was visible. What they had done with the mercenaries' bodies she couldn't say and probably didn't want to know.

Rena had given both Willow and Justin hugs, much to their surprise. After a large exchange of phone numbers with Justin and his new family, he seemed to be taking it in stride. She glanced through the open doorway at Justin where he talked to Finn in the front yard.

What will I do? She had no idea. "I'm not sure. You must be looking forward to going home finally."

Cory sighed. "I am. Finn too. I miss my family." She put her hand on Willow's arm. "I never asked. I should have. I've been too wrapped up in my own head. How are you dealing with all of this? He was your father."

Willow shook her head. "He wasn't. He may have contributed to my genetic makeup, but he wasn't a father."

"Still. You must have some conflicted feelings about what happened here."

"Maybe it's wrong or hard to understand, but all I feel about his death is relief. The weight of constant fear is suddenly gone."

Cory rubbed her arm. "Of course it's not wrong, I just want to make sure you're okay."

Willow hugged her. "I am, and thank you. You're a good friend. I've never had one of those before, so I appreciate that you care."

"No matter what you decide, know I'm here for you. You can call and chat or come for a nice long visit while you decide your next steps. You and Justin are always welcome. I hope you know that."

Willow forced a smile. Cory assumed whatever decision she made would include Justin. Unfortunately, she didn't share that confidence. "Thank you."

They walked outside and joined the men milling about by the path's opening. Willow gave Finn a hug goodbye before watching him and Cory disappear down the trail.

When will I see them again? It was a bit strange how close they had become in such a short time, but maybe it was because of the intensity and danger they'd all endured together. They'd formed bonds.

"We should head out, too, Willow."

She stared at her brother, deeply aware of Justin standing behind her. *Will he say anything? Is that what he wants too? For me to leave with Sebastian?* She had made a promise to Justin not to get attached. She'd assured him she could handle walking away.

"Willow, can we talk?"

Tension invaded every cell of her body. *Is this goodbye?*

Sebastian frowned. "Make it brief. We need to get on the road."

Willow turned and glanced at Justin. She couldn't discern his thoughts from his expression.

"Walk with me?"

She followed him across the yard in silence. If he wanted to say goodbye, then she wouldn't make it hard on him. A promise was a promise. It wasn't his fault her heart was breaking. Tears filled her eyes, but she forced them back. She would not crumble in front of him.

He walked into the trees. Ferns brushed her ankles, and the air grew cooler under the canopy of towering redwoods. They walked until the cabin disappeared from view behind them.

Justin stopped by a fallen branch that stood wider than the two of them together. "Do you want to sit?"

She climbed onto the log and braced herself for whatever goodbye speech he'd prepared. The wood was hard beneath her palms. She dug her nails into the bark, desperate for some distraction from the pain and grief. It felt like a death. Maybe that was her punishment for feeling no sadness over Edward's demise.

Justin rubbed the back of his neck and stared at the ground. She should probably say something to make it easier on him, but if she opened her mouth, she might beg him to give their relationship a chance.

"Do you want to leave with Sebastian?"

Her head shot up. "What?"

"I asked if you want to leave with him. He said the two of you are going to his house in Connecticut."

Had he? Sebastian hadn't discussed it with her. In fact, he'd never even asked her what she wanted to do. She guessed he had assumed she would go wherever he went.

"Is that what you want?"

What is he asking? Is he giving me another option? Does he want me to stay—with him? Maybe he was only concerned she might not realize she had other options besides staying with her brother. She did. She could travel alone. With the threat of Edward no longer breathing down her neck, she could do all the things she had only ever dreamed of. But none of them filled her with happiness any longer. It all felt empty. She felt empty.

Willow swallowed hard and looked anywhere but at Justin. "I made you a promise, Justin, and I'm trying very hard to keep it."

"What promise?"

"To not ask you for more." She turned her head away as she lost the battle to hold her tears back and they spilled down her cheeks.

"And what if I want more?" His fingers grasped her chin and turned her head back to him. "I don't want you to go."

"What are you saying?"

He wiped the tears from her cheeks and cupped her face in his palms. "I'm saying that the thought of you leaving is driving me insane. I'm saying that you've not only given me a family, but you've taught me how to trust. You've taught me how to believe in a better life for myself, a life I didn't believe possible. Just thinking of you provides me with an anchor to control my destructive powers. You calm me. You give me hope. I love you, Willow. Please give us a chance."

Willow sobbed as she threw herself into his arms. *He loves me.*

His arms held her tight as she wrapped herself around him and let all the tears pour onto his shoulder.

Justin loves me!

"I'm really hoping this means you feel the same and you're not crying because you don't know how to tell me you feel differently. Some words would be helpful, Willow."

She gasped and shook her head violently. *How could he possibly doubt my feelings?* Scrubbing her wet cheeks, she raised her head and gave him a wobbly smile. "I love you so much. It was killing me to walk away and not tell you."

He kissed her. "Thank you, God!"

She giggled and kissed him. "How could you think I wanted to leave?"

"This whole relationship thing is kind of new to me. I didn't want to pressure you so soon after everything went down, but then Sebastian sprang it on me that you were leaving, and I panicked."

"Relationships are new to me too. How about we make a new promise to one another that we always tell each other how we feel so there are no misunderstandings?"

Justin rested his forehead against hers, his hands supporting her body. "Agreed." His eyes gazed into hers. "I love you. I really thought I would never say those words to a woman, let alone feel them. But they're surprisingly easy to say to you. In fact, I really like saying them. I love you."

Willow laughed. "I can't believe how happy I am!" She tightened her arms around his neck. "I love you so much." Joy filled the very core of her being. She loved and was loved in return.

All the magic in the world couldn't compare to that feeling.

EPILOGUE

"I'm engaged!" Cory's excited voice conveyed her happiness even over the phone.

Willow gasped. "Oh my stars!"

Justin looked up from his tablet across the hotel room. She smiled to let him know it was good news.

"Congratulations! Tell me everything."

Cory laughed. "You won't believe what he did. I was running late for work, so I may have been speeding a little. I wasn't entirely surprised to see the police lights in the rearview mirror or hear the siren. All I was thinking about was the new arrangement of plants I wanted to build by the sign for the greenhouses, ya know?"

Willow chuckled. "I can imagine. I can't wait to see your place when we visit next month."

Cory had bought her old workplace from her bosses. They still helped out with the transition, but they were enjoying their retirement. She was looking forward to seeing Sebastian as well. Their phone calls had become brief lately. Something was up with her brother and she intended to find out what.

. . .

"O, wait until you see it. It's fantastic. And now that Mel has moved here, we're having a blast. But I digress. So there I was, thinking up possible excuses for the police officer and hoping I could wheedle out of a ticket because, wouldn't you know it, just that morning, Finn had lectured me on my driving."

"You must have loved that."

"Not the least little bit, and I made sure he knew it by weaving a little spell that covered his car in weeds before I left."

"You didn't." Willow covered her mouth with her free hand.

Justin quirked a brow at her, and she winked. The ocean glistened under the afternoon sun outside their balcony doors. The waves crashed on the beach below. They were in paradise, or more specifically, Hawaii. He'd taken her very seriously when she'd said she wanted to see the world. She had set foot on every continent. She was a long way from the girl who'd only visited places in the stories she read.

"Oh, I definitely did." Cory chuckled. "Anyway, the officer approached the car, and I lowered my window and babbled an apology. All I heard was license and registration, so I opened the glove compartment, and instead of finding the paperwork I prayed was in there, out fell a ring box. I must have stared stupidly at it for a solid minute." Cory sighed dreamily. "My car door opened, and I turned to glare at the officer. I mean, I was ready to blast him into next week. I didn't know if it was some evil witch impersonating a cop or what. I just knew a real cop wouldn't open my door like that. So, I whipped my head around, and there was Finn, dressed in a cop's uniform, down on one knee. My heart stopped in my chest as he removed the police cap and sunglasses."

Willow drew in a sharp breath. "I did not see that coming."

"Me either. I had been so busy coming up with excuses, I never really saw him as he approached my car. I looked at him then back at the ring, and I swear my jaw came unhinged it dropped so low. I had no idea he was going to propose."

"Aw."

"I know, right? I started bawling as soon as he opened his mouth. He had to repeat the question three times."

"That's so perfect for the two of you. I couldn't be happier for you, and no couple is more deserving than you two."

"Oh, I don't know about that. I'll be expecting a phone call from you soon."

Willow smiled. The thought of Justin proposing to her someday gave her a nice little hitch in the chest. "Someday."

"Oh, listen, I've got to go. Mel just pulled up with the last of her things from New Jersey, and I want to show her my ring. I can't wait to see you next month. Talk soon."

Willow chuckled as she said goodbye and the phone disconnected. She turned her head to tell Justin the good news. "In case you couldn't guess, Cory and Finn are engaged. He pretended to be a police officer and..."

Justin stood next to her with a ring in the palm of his hand.

That cannot mean what I think it means. Why is Justin holding a diamond ring?

"It was my grandmother's. I never thought I'd find anyone I wanted to give it to. I've been trying to plan something romantic, but it's just not in my wheelhouse, I guess. I had planned to ask you over dinner tonight on the beach, but I don't want to wait. I love you, Willow. More every single day. I'd like nothing better than to have you be my wife. Will you marry me?"

Willow stared at him. She'd lost the power of speech. She heard roaring in her ears. Justin wavered and disappeared from her vision.

A green lawn appeared before her. A little boy and girl played with a brown-and-white puppy. They laughed and giggled as the three danced around. Tears filled her eyes. There wasn't a doubt in her mind that the children were hers. Hers and Justin's.

The little boy and girl both turned to her and smiled. "Hi, Mommy," they chorused.

Willow glanced over her shoulder, but no one was there. She turned back as they both giggled.

They see me?

The boy waved, and the little girl blew her a kiss as the vision faded before her eyes.

"Willow?" Justin kneeled in front of her. His concerned gaze filled her sight.

She laughed and wiped the tear trickling down her nose.

"Where did you go?"

"I saw our children. They saw me too."

Justin smiled. "Does that mean your answer is yes?"

Willow laughed and hugged him. "A thousand times yes!"

THANK you for reading *Legacy of Destruction*! I hope you enjoyed Willow and Justin's story. *Legacy of Deceit*, Sebastian's story is next! If you haven't read the first book in the series, *Legacy of Magic*, you can read Cory and Finn's story now.

BE sure to check out my other book, *Bloodlines*, for another paranormal romance!

SIGN up for my newsletter to be the first to hear about new releases, sales, giveaways, and exclusive offers.

Acknowledgments

There are many reasons this book took so long to release. I won't list them here, but I do want to thank everyone for their patience. I always intended to continue the Legacy series and there are more on the way. *Legacy of Deceit,* Sebastian's story, is already in the works.

I want to thank my editor, Amanda Kruse, for not only catching all my oopsies (and there are a lot of them), but having the unique ability to make a manuscript better without compromising an author's voice.

Thank you to all of those at Red Adept Editing who had a hand in working on my manuscript!

Family is everything and without mine I wouldn't be able to do what I love.

I want to thank all the readers from the bottom of my heart. Your kind words and continued interest in the stories swirling around in my mind are what keep me motivated to keep sharing them!

Thank you for reading Legacy of Destruction! I hope you enjoyed Willow and Justin's story.

About the Author

Denise Carbo writes immersive, happily-ever-after Romance and Women's Fiction with a touch of humor and suspense. She is a voracious reader, loves to travel, and is fascinated by the supernatural.

She lives in a small, picturesque, New England town with her high school sweetheart and their three amazing sons. Find out more at https://www.DeniseCarbo.com and sign up for her newsletter to be the first to hear about new books, sales, giveaways, and exclusive content. https://eepurl.com/dt5N7M

ALSO BY DENISE CARBO

Bloodlines

Clan. Duty. Love. Which will he choose?

They have been here for centuries. War destroyed their planet, and now they hide among us. Malcolm Donovan, a dragon shifter, rules over one of four clans. When a clan member is murdered, he must find the killer. Nothing will disrupt his pledge to protect his clan. Nothing that is until he finds his mate.

Elsie Monroe, human to the bone, and the resort manager for the Donovan family finds herself falling in love with the charming Wyoming town, and she can't help but be drawn to the mysterious Malcolm Donovan. His rude attitude is atrocious, but his kisses can bring chocolate to a boiling point. Not to mention what he does to her body and heart.

Soon Elsie is dragged into a world of secrecy and violence. Creatures she thought were fantasy are actually real. And she is left wondering if love will be enough to capture and tame her own personal dragon.

Guilt & Redemption

Allison is a widow with dark secrets. Nightmares plague her nights. Guilt and shame shadow her days. Her new neighbor sparks feelings she thought shriveled and dead.

Jim's temporary lifestyle of renovating a house, selling it, and moving on doesn't leave room for relationships—and that's just the way he likes it. His new neighbor is not his type, but he's drawn to her anyway.

Allison's past won't stay buried. Trust is a precious commodity. Revenge, truth, and justice all have two sides. Will Allison and Jim find themselves on opposing sides?

My First My Last My Only

A second chance at love or heartbreak...

Socially awkward and prone to accidents, Franny Dawson has a brand-new project—herself. Owning the local bakery, The Sweet Spot, has taken all her time and energy and she's neglected the social aspects of her life. The small lakeside town of Granite Cove, New Hampshire is full of quirky residents eager to help and hinder her new plan.

Mitch Atwater, her first love, returns to town. He has an agenda of his own and is wreaking havoc with her goals and her heart.

Can Franny outwit her nemesis, overcome her perfect sister's surprise return, and escape the cocoon of her own insecurities to take a chance on love and get her very own happily ever after?

Covet thy Neighbor

Serial killer or new love interest...

Single mom of twin boys, Olivia Banner, has her hands full juggling life's demands. She doesn't have time for her mysterious new neighbor or all the questions his presence conjures up, even if he is a handsome devil.

Toss in a complicated relationship with her ex-husband, meddlesome family members, and going back to school to provide a stable financial future for her and her boys, and Olivia turns to her gal pals for guidance.

Sometimes playing it safe is the right choice, and other times leaping into the unknown can lead to all the dreams you never knew you had coming true.

No Choice at All

One night. One choice. Changes everything.

One single moment can change a person's life forever. Moving to Granite Cove was supposed to be Rebecca's fresh start. She has a firm no dating rule. There's no time or room in her life—*and* she has horrible taste in men.

One impulsive decision threatens all her careful planning. Ian, the handsome stranger she never thought she'd see again, keeps showing up and weakening her resolve.

Love is a fairy tale only the young and naïve believe in. Can Ian change her mind and heart and teach her to trust?

Whispers & Broken Promises

Dumped and deserted...

Instead of the proposal she expected, Tina's boyfriend dumps her and moves across the country. She's left behind questioning her future and what went wrong.

A handsome single dad moves to town and the complications multiply.

She's spent her entire existence in the small lakeside town of Granite Cove, New Hampshire. Besides knowing every detail of her life, the residents feel it's only right they help her decide how she should live the rest of it.

A Yearning Dilemma

Kelly yearns for a family connection despite being surrounded by siblings, parents, and extended relations. She let chance choose her destiny and ended up in Granite Cove searching for a home.

A contrary celebrity ensnares her in the turmoil embroiling his life and makes her question all her choices.

Christmas is the season of miracles and forgiveness, but how do you choose between family, friends, career, and love? And why do you have to?

A Change in Perspective

What do you do when your perfect life blows up in your face? Move home to Granite Cove and hope you can put some of the pieces back together. Except what if the pieces no longer fit?

Lucinda reevaluates her life decisions and realizes many of her choices don't paint a pretty picture. She's determined to put her people pleasing habits behind her and discover the life she's meant to live.

She's known Bobby all her life—at least she thought she did. He keeps showing up at all the wrong times and making his dislike of her crystal clear.

Secrets and lies. Responsibilities and expectations. Betrayal and loss. Can love really heal all wounds?